Forbidden by the Bratva

Dad's Best Friend Mafia Romance

Morozov Bratva Book 5

Lexi Asher

CONTENTS

CHAPTER 1 - EVELINA

Sitting in the busy coffee shop in Brooklyn, I felt a prickle of awareness run down my spine. I took a sip of my frothy cappuccino, the best one I'd ever had, and casually glanced around. No one seemed out of the ordinary, and the other customers were completely absorbed in their drinks or devices. Or each other. Against my will, I smiled at a couple utterly wrapped up in themselves, clearly wildly in love. Lucky them.

I didn't have time for fleeting envy and kept perusing the area for whatever might have tweaked my fight-or-flight response.

Outside the window, mostly covered in pastel paint advertising the café's specials, no one was hanging around, peering in, or even pausing in their steady march along the sidewalk. I was most likely being paranoid, but it wasn't without reason.

My father was the head of the most prominent crime family in Moscow, and my cousin Ivan was the head of the Miami branch of the Morozov empire. There were a lot of people who wanted to kill both of them on a regular basis and, by extension, anyone who was related to them. Being on my guard, even at low-risk places like coffee shops, kept me alive for twenty-four years. By now, it was just a habit to be aware of my surroundings and listen to my gut.

That instinct seemed to alert me to something, but I must have been imagining things this time. I settled back in with my coffee, enjoying the short break I was allowing myself from work.

About a month ago, I did a favor for my cousin Yuri, and he let my brother and I come to the US as thanks for our expertise. Miami Beach was fantastic, and living with Yuri and his new wife, Kira, who quickly became one of my best friends, was great. The perfect weather, the luxe mansion, the nightclubs, and the parties were experiences I savored, especially since it was so different from Moscow. But I quickly became bored.

I craved work even more than I wanted caffeine first thing in the morning. Maybe more since I usually checked my computer before hitting the Keurig machine button. Back home, I had a thriving private investigation company, along with whatever my father wanted me to do for the family business. I rarely would have had time for glittering parties or just lying out on the sand.

Sure, there were more serious things to do in Miami. Ivan and my other cousins were thrilled to have my brother's prowess in coding and mine in surveillance, and I was more than happy to lend a hand. Family was always going to be the most important thing to me. I was proud of my father and my cousins and the power they had amassed. Still, no matter what I did, I couldn't make them see I was ready to be a leader. That there were new territories ripe for the picking. Which was why I decided to strike out on my own. To prove my mettle, to myself and to them.

When my oldest and very best friend Kristina found out I was on this side of the pond and invited me to New York, I jumped at the chance, already researching the families here before I even ended the call with her.

We were always as thick as thieves, constantly making both our fathers tear their hair out. While her father had a thick, full head of it, my poor Papa ended up nearly bald because of our antics. We hadn't seen each other in almost two years but had kept in constant contact anyway, and it was like no time had passed when she greeted me at the airport. In fact, she was already complaining about the huge delivery of boxes that had arrived the day before me, shaking her head that I was about to cram all my computer equipment into her tiny apartment.

Kristina had come to New York City to try her hand at acting after we both graduated college. She'd always been active in drama clubs and community theater. Still, I figured she'd give it up and go into the family business like I did. She could have had ample acting roles on Russian television on the side with her father's influence, but she wanted to prove she had enough talent to make it on her own in the States. Two days after I landed, she got a role in a show filmed in New England somewhere, leaving me alone for the rest of the week.

The coffee shop door swung open with its tinkling bell, and I felt the odd prickle again but blew it off. No one involved with the Bratva knew where I was except for my twin, Leo, and that was only because he helped me with his genius hacking and coding skills. The update he sent me should have been fully installed by now, so it was time to get back to work.

I got back in line to buy a pastry and another of their god-tier cappuccinos, then headed back to Kristina's apartment. It was small but luxurious compared to what many so-called starving artists had to live in around here. Even though her dad didn't exactly approve of her choices, he still helped her out a lot and would have taken a bullet before letting her stay in a rat trap. Probably only her fierce independence kept her from accepting a penthouse in Manhattan.

The cozy place, decorated in sparse modern style and scattered with glossy headshots and scripts, was way more my speed than my cousins' giant mansions. I settled in comfortably at the desk I'd commandeered with all my monitors and machines.

Now, I hated to call what I was doing spying, but it was essentially spying. The Novikoffs was an upstart family from Saint Petersburg who would never have crossed my radar if they hadn't started encroaching on territory that we'd—well, my cousins—had taken over in Boston. They'd really dug in here in NYC, an area my cousins had started musing about branching into since Boston had proven to be so lucrative.

The more I learned about the Novikoffs, the more I was impressed by the power and riches they'd gained in a short amount of time, and the more I wanted to take them down. Not just because they were causing trouble for my family but because this was my chance to prove I could run an area on my own.

My father was firm but fair with both my brother and me, but there was always the unspoken assumption that it would be Leo who inherited the keys to our kingdom in Moscow, and I'd continue to assist. No matter that Leo was content with his nose stuck in his code. Yes, he was prepared to stand up and do what he needed to do, but he'd be more than happy to concede to me. Not just out of love and loyalty but because he could see I was the right choice.

I was always the one with the ambition and drive—hell, I'd had my investigation company up and running before my first year of college and managed to do both, along with whatever family business arose, with ease. If I'd been a man, Papa would have surely seen what Leo could, but our father was old-fashioned and set in his ways. In his mind, I'd eventually get married and give up all my "hobbies" to settle down and raise the next generation of Morozovs.

Like hell.

The software update was complete, and I logged onto all the cameras I'd been able to hack into since I got here. So far, I had control of cameras at six of the Novikoff's businesses, but none seemed to be where they had their most important meetings. It didn't matter. I was on it, and everything they owned would soon be in my control.

Before I got back to work in earnest, my eyes settled on the framed picture that had been pushed to the back of the desk. It was a photo of college graduation two years ago, and Kristina and I both glowed with happiness and pride in our black caps and gowns. I wasn't looking at either of us but at the man who stood in the middle, towering over us with a big, proud smile of his own, pulling us into a hug. If I closed my eyes and drifted back in time, I could still feel that firm hand on my shoulder, burning through the flimsy synthetic graduation gown and my pristine white dress underneath.

Kristina was my dearest friend. We'd been drawn to each other in elementary school due to our similar rambunctious personalities and the fact that we'd both lost our mothers at a young age. Mine to a terrible disease, while hers had just up and left. We were as close as sisters, and that man in the photo had raised me almost as much as my own father.

But I'd never once thought of him like that. How could I, with all the other thoughts I had about him? Innocent enough when I was ten—he'd been a hero to me then. Not so innocent in my teen years, but I'd kept my wild crush well hidden. Kristina would have teased me mercilessly before beating me up, and I would have died of shame if she—or God forbid—he ever found out.

"Concentrate," I growled, tipping the picture forward so I couldn't be distracted by it.

Kristina had cleared everything off of the desk for me when we set up my equipment, but something made me put the picture back. The crush was long gone now that I was an adult, and I could handle the memories.

"Apparently not, though." I laughed at myself, nearly lapsing into one of my many old fantasies. I didn't have time for that, not if I wanted to prove to everyone that I could do far more than the surveillance jobs they gave me.

Work soon consumed me, the way I liked it, blocking everything out but my quest for information. My fingers flew over the keyboard as I took down notes, and my eyes were grainy and glazed over when the sound of my phone pulled me out of my trance. Swearing and rubbing my eyes, I saw it was Leo, which was odd since we mostly just texted unless it was an emergency.

"What?" I answered. My twin didn't need any niceties from me. "Do you have something good for me? Because I'm—"

"Evelina shut up and listen," he rumbled. Usually, his voice brought a smile to my face, but his tone just then sounded furious.

"What did I do?" I asked, wracking my brain. He wasn't quick to take offense to anything; we'd barely spoken in the last few days.

"Are you fucking kidding me?" he answered.

What a minute. He didn't sound pissed; he sounded scared, even more rare from Leo. "What's going on? Is something wrong with Papa?"

"The fact that what you're up to is going to give him a heart attack," he snapped. "But that's not why I'm calling. You need to get back to Miami right away. Now. While we're talking, I need you to start getting your ass to the airport."

"Will you calm down and explain to me what's got you sounding like—"

"Like my fucking sister's trying to get herself killed?" he interrupted, taking a few seconds to swear under his breath before continuing.

I asked him as calmly as I could what he was on about, feigning all sorts of innocence because Leo knew where I was but not what I was trying to do. It seemed like he'd somehow found out.

"Can the act," he said. "If I knew what you were really doing, I never would have helped you."

"Sure, you would have," I said, trying to get him to sound normal. "So, yeah. I've been hacking into the Novikoff's security cameras and keeping an eye on them."

"And they're onto you, Ev. Papa's going out of his mind and blaming me as if I'm responsible for your hare-brained schemes."

Well, that stung, but I brushed it off. Getting a dressing down from our father wasn't pleasant, to say the least. "I'm sorry, but you are four minutes older," I teased.

"Are you not hearing me?" he roared as loudly as the king of the jungle he was named for. "They're onto you. The operation is over. Come back to Miami or go home, but you can't stay in New York anymore."

"Leo, I've been watching them, listening to their conversations. Nobody's onto me. Papa's information is incorrect."

He swore some more, and there was a long silence on both sides, a Morozov twin impasse that happened when neither of us wanted to concede.

"You're out of your depth on this one," he finally said. "And I'm not helping you anymore."

I looked down at my phone, stunned that he had hung up on me. Hurt that he didn't think I could handle myself. Irritation grew, and I tossed the phone onto the desk, shoving everything aside except for my main mission. Take down the Novikoffs and make their territory my own. The fire was even stronger now that their existence was bothering my father. I didn't like him to worry about me, but I was certain nothing was awry.

Leo would come around. He always did. Still, that odd prickle of awareness I felt at the coffee shop returned to the front of my mind. Maybe I should listen to him, after all.

A ping from my computer drew my attention to the main monitor. I had another camera come online, showing a small, seedy bar interior. Three men huddled at a booth, deep in concentration. Enlarging the view, I couldn't hold back a grin, despite my trepidation from mere seconds ago.

The head of the Novikoffs was gesticulating across the table at the others. Were they arguing over the best vodka, or was this the place they held their most important meetings? The only way to find out was to get the exact location—piece of cake—and go there and plant some bugs. Not easy, but doable. I had years of experience lurking around undercover, and my actress best friend had plenty of wigs and makeup.

I getting closer. No way I could give up because our dad heard something that spooked him and then yelled at Leo. I knew how to be careful, and I'd be even more cautious now that I'd been warned of a possible threat to my operation.

It was time to pick out a wig because I wasn't about to give up just because my father and my four-minutes-older brother told me to.

Chapter 2 - Mikhail

This was my much-needed and long-awaited vacation, so it was a mystery why I was so tense. I had landed in New York only a few hours before to surprise my only daughter after not seeing her for nearly a year. Things weren't exactly strained between us, but ever since she moved here to chase her crazy dreams, we definitely hadn't seen eye to eye.

I probably should have gone down to the islands and slept for three days straight because as much as I wanted to see her, it would be anything but relaxing. I'd just ended a long campaign to retrieve stolen territory from a brand-new organization that sorely underestimated the Russian Bratva. My mistake had been trying diplomacy with them, drawing lines and expecting my rules to be followed. They crossed my lines one too many times and learned what my swift and total retribution looked like. A lot of cleanup was necessary after it was all over—literal and figurative. Yes, I needed this vacation, no matter how short and no matter that I'd probably spend most of it arguing with my daughter.

Suddenly the bloody memories of the recent war didn't seem so harrowing with what I was about to face.

I had my driver drop me off a few blocks from Kristina's apartment; not sure if I shouldn't have called ahead. The neighborhood was a good one and a far cry from what she could have afforded alone. I never babied her, but like any parent, I only wanted her to be happy, and safety was always a top priority. It had to be in my line of work.

I was a powerful man—both here in the US and in our home country of Russia. That came with enemies, more than the ordinary successful businessman might have. Many more. So, of course, I couldn't let her live in some squalid walk-up with no security, even though I'd never be convinced that acting was the right path for her.

She didn't see it, but I was positive she could do great things in the family business and was sure she'd get the acting bug out of her system after enough rejections. My main worry was that she'd fall in love with an American and completely forget where she came from and who she was.

I spied a coffee shop across the street and grabbed a cup to help steady my nerves. The fact I could hunt down an assassin or drive violent interlopers out of my territories without breaking a sweat, but a surprise visit to my daughter twisted my stomach in knots was something I'd never really understood.

It was rough being a single dad, but I wouldn't have changed a thing, even though her mother tried to destroy me when she ran out on us when Kristina was only ten.

Kristina never said it in so many words, but she clearly blamed me and my position in the Bratva for her mother's unhappiness and the ultimate reason she left. Never mind that the wretched woman never acknowledged Kristina again or tried to contact her after she took off. If she hadn't given me my daughter, I would have regretted every minute with her.

It would have taken very little evidence to show Kristina the truth about her mother and all her perfidy, but I held my tongue. I would have put up with the constant cheating, the stealing, and the lies if only she'd been a good mother. But she wasn't. She'd been cold and resentful of Kristina and probably would have ended up doing a great deal of damage to her self-esteem if she'd stuck around.

So, I never said a word against her, even though it put all the blame squarely on me. It didn't matter as long as my little girl could cling to the illusion that she had a mother who loved her.

Okay, so maybe I babied her a little.

I settled in at a corner table with my espresso to people-watch in the bustling city I hadn't been to in far too long. The last time I saw Kristina was Christmas the year before when I dragged her back to Moscow under the threat of cutting off her rent here. Despite splitting my time between Moscow and the glittering jewel of Miami Beach, she'd only visited me there once, and that was in passing while on location for some modeling job. It was time to put my foot down, set a timeline for her to fulfill her American dreams, and then return to reality.

But the minute I saw her, I'd cave and probably buy her a car or something equally foolish, which was why I was whiling away my precious vacation time in a coffee shop before knocking on her door.

Looking around at the quirky decor, a glossy flash of red hair caught my eye. Moving my gaze downward, that shock of long, silky auburn hair flowed down a curvy backside. Black jeans molded to lush hips and an ass that made my hands twitch in anticipation of cupping each cheek. I leaned forward to get a better view of this beauty, hoping she'd sit close enough to me that I could easily strike up a conversation. Hell, I'd move tables if I had to.

I was on vacation, after all. Why not have a little fun of my own in between visits with Kristina?

My phone buzzed furiously, drawing my attention down long enough to see it was my old friend Oleg Morozov. One could say he was a rival—we often butted heads over whose territory was who's both in Moscow and Miami, but his daughter and mine had been the best of friends and thick as thieves since they met in their last year of elementary school.

Their friendship had forced two families together that might have destroyed one another if there wasn't that common ground. Oleg was as much of a sucker for his kids as I was, and over the years, he and I had become quite chummy with each other. Commiserating over vodka shots about our children's mishaps over the last fourteen years created a solid bond between us.

As I answered, my gaze trailed back to the gorgeous redhead. I barely heard Oleg's greeting when she turned around. Then everything about her except the long red hair was familiar. Too familiar. The bright, intelligent green eyes, high cheekbones, and full lips currently covered in too much dark lipstick for my taste but did nothing to mar their sensuous outline. Her faded black t-shirt was covered by a black leather vest she'd cinched in to accentuate her very ample breasts.

I jerked my eyes back up, and my jaw nearly hit the speckled Formica table top because the last person I expected to see was Evelina Morozov—Kristina's best friend and Oleg's daughter. I quickly turned so she wouldn't see me as she left with her order.

I probably shouldn't have been so shocked. The two girls were always inseparable, and I was only a block from Kristina's apartment. As Evelina left with her order, I was unable to keep from watching the sway of those hips as she sauntered out.

She'd always been a beautiful girl. I'd had to step way back on more than one occasion to keep things appropriate. I hadn't seen her in two years, and the woman I couldn't tear my eyes from now was all grown up, with a body that wouldn't stop.

Holy shit, what was I thinking? With her father on the phone, no less. I should have been horsewhipped. If she had seen me, there was no doubt she'd have recognized what I'd been thinking since I hadn't cooled off from all the plans I'd been building up in my mind after I worked my charms on her. When I still thought she was a sexy stranger, that was. Not Oleg's daughter.

"What's up, Oleg?" I asked, unaccountably still shaken by the strength of my feelings. "You'll never believe this, but I just clapped eyes on Evelina. Small world, eh?"

Oleg babbled in an incoherent mix of English and Russian, and I realized he was panicking about something. It only got worse when I mentioned Evelina.

"Where are you?" he demanded. "Is she okay?"

"I'm in New York," I answered. "And yes, she seemed fine. I didn't say hello to her because I don't want Kristina to know I'm here until I figure out—"

"Listen, Mikhail, she's in trouble," he said. My staid friend seemed to be on the verge of tears. "She's meddling in something way over her head, and now she's in too deep. The Novikoffs have put a hit out on her."

The second he said she was in trouble, I immediately ditched my coffee and stood, leaving the shop. Heading toward Kristina's apartment at a brisk pace, but one that wouldn't raise eyebrows, I soon spotted Evelina at a magazine kiosk, picking out some snacks. Despite my worry over what Oleg had just told me, I couldn't help but smile, remembering how she always needed a steady flow of fuel when she and Kristina pulled all-night study sessions.

"I'm on her, Oleg. Calm down and tell me what's going on."

"She refuses to stop poking the hornet's nest. You've got to get her out of New York," he pleaded. "Take her with you to Miami until I can come to collect her. Leo can't make her see reason, and she won't take my calls, so I can't order her to stop."

I sighed, keeping my distance when Evelina started walking again but never letting her out of my sight. Still as stubborn as ever, it seemed.

"If she won't listen to her brother, she's certainly not going to listen to me."

"I don't want you to talk to her," he said, exasperated.

"I'm only here for a few days. I don't know what—"

He broke in, his voice rising. "My daughter is in danger, Mikhail! You need to act." He ended his demand on a shout.

I bristled. I never took orders from a Morozov, friend or no friend. I never took orders from anyone. But Evelina was… well, I wouldn't say she was like a daughter. Not after the way I'd been thinking about her in the coffee shop. I would be devastated, though, if the unspeakable happened to her. Kristina would be broken if she lost her best friend.

"I'll see what I can do." I ended the call on his rush of thanks.

I swore as I followed Evelina at a short distance until she was safely inside Kristina's building. It was easy enough to get past those key-coded doors. Even easier to take out a doorman after you scare him into telling you the correct apartment number. If someone was determined to take Evelina down, the flimsy security that gave me enough peace of mind to let Kristina stay, there was really no security at all. I had to believe the only reason they hadn't come after her yet was because they hadn't found her. But if they wanted her that badly, they would. It was only a matter of time.

I swore some more, calling for my driver to meet me so I could formulate a plan.

So much for my vacation.

CHAPTER 3 - EVELINA

I got into the apartment and caught a glimpse of myself in the hall mirror. Flipping the long, red tresses behind my shoulder, I grinned at my reflection. I must have been more like Kristina than I thought because I loved wearing a different wig every day. I usually kept my dark hair in a simple bob that never reached my shoulders, making it easy to stuff it under hats when I was undercover. Still, I could get used to the wig life.

I set my coffee and snacks next to my keyboard, a bit miffed that I couldn't sit and relax in the shop for a bit between work sessions. It was lonely and insufferable being cooped up in Kristina's apartment without her, but I had been taking my brother's warning seriously, only leaving for short periods and always in disguise. Leo wouldn't be placated, though, and still refused to speak to me, only sending me daily messages to get my ass home.

Well, I didn't take orders from my brother. I was dodging my father's calls so he couldn't give me an order I'd have to follow or risk a far more serious outcome than getting my twin's cold shoulder.

Once I cracked the Novikoff's most secret information, I'd be the one giving orders, and both Leo and our dad would see I was right all along. I settled in and put my earbuds in, ready to take notes on the most recent surveillance footage I'd gathered. I had run into a few snags that took much more time than they should have to iron out without Leo's help, but I was no slouch in the hacking department and was managing just fine without him.

If only they weren't so overprotective! I loved that about both of them; knew it was bred deep into their bones to care for the women they loved, but it could be annoying when I only wanted to spread my wings and fly.

Not much was going on today on my screens or in my earbuds. I had managed to pose as a lost tourist in a curly blonde wig and oversized sunglasses to get into the bar where I'd seen the Novikoff head and his men arguing. I just waited around in a hired taxi, assuring the driver, who was bored out of his skull, that I really didn't want to go anywhere, and watched them on the remote access feed on my phone until they cleared out. After that, it was easy to slide into the booth next to the one they'd been in and stick my listening device under the table while the bartender mixed me up a Long Island iced tea and tried to give me directions.

Out of habit, while I worked, I turned around to crack a joke with Leo, who, of course, wasn't there, and with a sigh, went back to staring at the screens. Kristina's walk-on role had been expanded, and she was staying up north for a few extra days. Since she made friends everywhere, she went, the cast and crew invited her to the weekly wrap party after the episode was finished so she wouldn't be home for the weekend, either.

I wasn't what anyone would call an extrovert, but I was used to working closely with Leo or the employees at my detective firm. The past month I'd been living with my cousin Yuri and his wife Kira and had started looking forward to always having friendly faces around. There was always something exciting to do in Miami and plenty to do here in New York. But if I went out and did any of it and got myself killed, my brother would gloat about it at my funeral and say that he was right.

I tossed my earbuds onto the desk and rolled my shoulders. It was time to admit I was a little bit lonely. I needed a break if the creaking sound from my neck was any indication. Nothing was happening, and I was recording everything anyway.

I decided to slip on the blonde wig and go out for a quick walk around the nearby park. As usual, I slid my small 9 mm pistol into the back waistband of my jeans and pulled my vest down to conceal it. That concession wasn't for my father and brother. That was just common sense in my life.

After I nodded at the doorman and pushed through the doors to get some much-needed fresh air—well, as fresh as it got in New York—I was shocked to see it was dark out. I pulled my phone out to see it was after eight. No wonder all my vertebrae were locked up, and my eyes were dry and grainy. Time often got away from me when I got into the zone with my work, but I didn't want to go back in. This was a good neighborhood, the streets were well-lit, and I was armed. I needed some exercise, so I decided to just take a fast jaunt to the park and around the sandy running track once. Then back to safety—and loneliness.

That's the price of getting what you want.

I could go back to Miami or Moscow at any time and give up this project, but I felt it would be my last shot at proving what I was capable of. Not just to my father but to myself. I knew I could lead because I'd been taught by the best, and it was what I wanted more than anything. I'd be shuffled back into a supporting role if I left now. An important one, but not enough for me. Was it so wrong to want more?

I snorted as I stomped along the sidewalk, pretty sure Leo didn't constantly question his motives. He was much more easygoing than I was and less ambitious. If my father could have switched our personalities, I was sure he would have. It just pissed me off that he couldn't see that he didn't have to, and it hurt more than a little that I wasn't enough as I was.

A sleek sedan with darkly tinted windows rolled up slowly alongside me, and I jerked out of my troubled musings. I had a supposed hit on me, for God's sake. I needed to keep my wits about me. Veering off the sidewalk, I cut across an empty lot to get to the park. As soon as I was beyond the small gate that led into the green space, I surreptitiously turned to watch the sedan keep cruising down the block and round the corner.

Breathing a sigh of relief and snickering over my paranoia, I headed toward the deserted swings. I used to love flying and pumping my legs to get higher. No one was around, so why not? Then I could pretend my rapidly beating heart was because I was having fun, not because I'd been spooked by some random person trying to get through the narrow streets.

But I didn't make it to the swings. No sooner had I gone around the wooden playscape that an arm snaked out from behind a slide and wrapped around my shoulders, drawing me back into a solid wall of flesh.

"Just relax, Evelina."

The fact he knew my name, but I didn't recognize his voice chilled me to the bone. Relax? Like hell. I grappled behind me for my gun, but he was faster, and I felt him pluck it from my waistband.

I elbowed him hard but barely drew a grunt. Kicked his shins which only made him jerk me like a rag doll. His arm moved from across my shoulders to up around my neck, slowly tightening. Stepping outside of the situation, I placed myself back in the hundreds of self-defense classes I used to take with Kristina on both our fathers' orders. This wasn't real, and I was well-trained to get myself out of the situation.

I slammed my head backward, expecting to feel the jarring thud and hear the crunch of his nose breaking, but it was like he expected me to do just that and only laughed a low, sinister chuckle. All while his arm grew tighter around my neck, he dragged me backward. Somewhere. Somewhere I didn't want to be.

This was real.

Panic made me claw uselessly at his iron grip, feeling weaker by the second. Sparks of light wavered in my peripheral vision. If he didn't let go soon, I would pass out. Then be at his mercy. Damn it, those swings might have been the last thing I saw if I didn't get free.

I had one option left, and I opened my mouth to scream with the little air I still had. But he seemed to know I would do that too and slapped his other meaty hand over my mouth. Everything around me was racing away as my vision tunneled, becoming a pinprick as he dragged me from the playground. I flailed against the suffocation and clung to that little bit of light I could still see.

Until it was gone.

***

I slowly came back around, first noticing my throat was sore as if I'd swallowed ten fiery shots of homemade vodka back-to-back. Panic hit first, then rage that my brother was right, though I didn't really think he'd gloat at my funeral. I kept my eyes closed, trying to assess the situation and determine if I could escape. I slowly moved my legs and found they were free, though I was covered by a blanket. A nice, fresh-smelling blanket, but maybe the Novikoffs were fastidious murderers? My hope increased until I carefully moved my arms. It plummeted when I found my left wrist zip-tied to something hard and smooth.

My head felt surprisingly free, and as I lay there pretending to still be asleep, I realized whoever had grabbed me had taken my wig off. They had to know for sure who I was before they put the bullet in my head. That made sense. But why was I still alive?

I opened one eye to see my wrist bound to a gleaming brass post. Crisp white linen blocked the rest of my view until I slightly tilted my head a bit. A crystal lamp sat atop a marble-topped bedside table, and the wall beyond it was papered in a tasteful cream brocade design.

Okay, why was I still alive and in such a luxurious prison?

I shifted again to take in more of my surroundings. A man in a dark gray suit sat at a highly polished wooden desk, but his back was to me, and all I could make out was a thick, dark mane of hair that brushed the top of his collar. He dwarfed the fancy, spindly-legged chair. Something about him was overwhelmingly familiar, but he didn't seem to be any of the men I'd been spying on for the last few days.

"I know you're awake," a voice that made my blood heat up in my veins said. That wryly amused tone was one I'd heard a thousand times before.

He slowly turned, and the blast from the past was utterly overwhelming, along with all the feelings I thought were long buried. They weren't buried deep enough, or I wouldn't have put his picture back on my workspace. And when he smiled at me, those feelings scrambled right out and smacked me in the heart. And other places.

Mikhail Roslov. My best friend's father.

God, he was still so gorgeous. More than ever, really. I thought if I could avoid him, he'd eventually stop being larger than life in my thoughts, but the fact was he was just plain larger than life. Tall, even sitting in that silly, ornate chair. Broad shoulders only accentuated by his tailored suit. The dark waves streaked with bronze from the sun were messy at his temples as if he'd been running his long fingers through them. Something he did when he was irritated or worried. And like always, I wanted to smooth it with my fingers, then cup his strong jaw and stare into his bottomless, espresso-colored eyes. My gaze fell on his lips, still smiling at me. How many dreams had I had about kissing those lips?

"Hello, Evelina. I've been talking to your father. Seems like you've been a bad girl."

Anger washed away my foolish lust, and I sat up, wrenching my bound wrist but hardly feeling the pain. The flicker of concern that crossed his handsome face didn't make me waver from my wrath.

This was going to ruin everything I'd been working toward! I was too close to letting Mikhail derail me now.

"You—" I sputtered, shooting a glare that would have sent most people cowering.

Still, that smile. "It's good to see you again, too."

No. I wouldn't be swayed, made to see reason or give in to his endless charm. My future was on the line. I gnashed my teeth at him and prepared to make him sorry he'd ever sided with my dad against me.

CHAPTER 4 - MIKHAIL

As a child, Evelina could take down a house with the force of her rages, and it looked like she was about to show me that nothing had changed. I couldn't blame her for being mad since I sent one of my guys to pick her up, but how she looked at me now showed me I had made the right decision. She was so stubborn she couldn't see reason even when her damn life was in danger, so brute force was the only answer.

As she opened her mouth, I watched her delicate eyebrows draw together over her piercing green eyes. She was about to start hollering the roof off the place. I hurried over and pressed my finger over those luscious lips, quickly pulling it away before she could bite it off.

"Don't bother screaming," I said. That was a big mistake. Now she looked more determined than ever to deafen the entire hotel. I shrugged, leaning close enough to smell her strawberry shampoo. "Or go ahead. Scream yourself hoarse if you want. I paid a lot for this suite and informed management that my guest might get noisy."

I was bluffing, but she bought it, snapping her mouth shut on a mere squeak. Her face grew red with even more rage than what she woke up with.

Since I had to spend the last half an hour watching over her, I wasn't in the best of moods either. Not just the fact my bodyguard and I had to take turns hauling her up the stairs to my hotel suite. Once she was laid out on the bed, there was far too much time to take in the skin-tight jeans clinging to hips I longed to mold my fingers to. The way her beautiful dark hair spilled across the pillow once I took that ridiculous blonde wig off made me envision knotting it into my hand and tugging her head back so I could better reach her smooth throat with my tongue. It was fucking annoying, and I finally threw a blanket over her body since I couldn't stop gaping at her.

No, she wasn't a little girl anymore. Far from it, I wouldn't let her start acting like one to get what she wanted. Right now, what I wanted was more important: to keep her alive.

I gave her a death glare right back to her, shaking my head at her sputtering outrage at having been bested. She always hated to lose. She rarely did, and if it had been one of Novikoff's people who grabbed her in the park, she might have gotten away. But I knew she'd be carrying and exactly how she'd fight since I was there to oversee most of her self-defense classes, along with Kristina.

All the women in the Roslov and Morozov families were well-equipped to care for themselves, but I had sent my guy out prepared. Knowledge was power, not to mention he was built like a mountain and had no qualms about doing whatever I ordered.

Yes, I knew a lot about Evelina, and being so close to her after so long, seeing the gorgeous woman she'd become, had me wanting to get to know her more. A lot more. The way her eyes seared into mine, so full of passion, even though I knew it was born from wrath, made me feel the usual iron grip on my self-control slipping away.

That couldn't happen. Not ever. I had a job to do. Keep my best friend's daughter safe, not trail my finger down the side of her cheek to her parted lips to part them further. Lean down and ravage that angry mouth until she whimpered and begged for more. It didn't help that she was still zip tied to the bed, her breasts straining against her top with every heaving breath she took. She would be at my mercy. Until I was at hers because I had a strong feeling, she'd give as good as she got.

Jesus Christ.

I hurriedly got up to grab a pair of scissors off the desk, snipping away her binding. There. No longer at my mercy. Didn't help much, which bothered me. Where was the control I prided myself in having? This little girl had me close to being weak in the knees, about to start fumbling for her bra so I could glimpse her ripe tits.

It had to stop, and now.

"So, you know why you're here, then?" I asked once I moved further away so I could cool down.

She sighed. "My dad's being overprotective as usual." She scowled and looked around the presidential suite. "Who was that big asshole who jumped me? I want to make sure I kick him in the balls if I see him again."

I tsked at her language, which only made her roll her eyes at me. "That was my bodyguard, and you won't get the chance. We're heading back to Miami, where I can hide you until the threat is neutralized."

Her eyes softened, and she looked at me while biting her lower lip. "I don't want you to waste your time, Mikhail. There's no threat. This is nothing."

I laughed at her blatant attempt to manipulate me. She knew me as well as I knew her. I'd have to be extra careful not to fall for her tricks. I quickly grew serious, shaking my head at her.

"It's not nothing. I looked into it, and nobody's overreacting. You have a widespread bounty on your head, not the kind where you get a neat and tidy bullet in your skull. Novikoff found out about your little surveillance operation and wants you brought in so he can teach you a lesson before the bullet. You've been around long enough to know what I'm talking about, Evelina."

Her pretty face lost all its color. At least she would finally take me seriously now and stop making a fuss, but I wasn't as pleased as I should have been when my scare tactic worked. She looked rattled to the core, probably remembering some of her own father's gruesome interrogations. I had to stand up and move away. Sitting two feet away from her on the bed wasn't far enough to quell the urge to reach out and soothe her fears away. If I was being honest with myself, I was dying to touch her—no reason necessary.

I needed to get that under control. Fast.

"I don't want to go back to Miami," she said. "I'm so close—"

The irritation at myself made me snap at her and cut her off. "You don't get a say." I pointed to the giant suitcase on the rack with my folded vacation clothes. "I can easily knock you out again and stuff you in that to get you on the plane if you insist on not cooperating."

Once again, I was bluffing, but she actually gave me a horrified look that cut me to the bone. As if she believed I'd ever put her in a suitcase.

And idiot that I was, I started to apologize when she jumped up and darted toward the door. She managed to get it open and out into the hall before I could react because I was so stunned she would try something like that.

When I got to the door, she fled past my confused bodyguard and toward the emergency stairs.

"Should I go after her?" he asked.

"Yes," I told him, raking my hands through my hair. "Try to be gentle this time."

We were on the top floor of a thirty-eight-story building. She wouldn't get far with Andre on her heels, but of course, she had to try. With a nod, he took off at an easy jog, slamming through the door after her. I probably should have gone, but I couldn't make myself get rough with her, and I knew she'd put up a fight. That was just Evelina, never giving up.

When I learned that she had managed to infiltrate the Novikoff organization far enough to get caught, I was impressed. She'd always been smart, but it seemed like her skills had become highly advanced over the past years. She had always desperately competed with her brother for Oleg's favor, even though Leo was totally unaware of any competition going on.

I would have felt a pang of sympathy for her having to give up all her hard work if it weren't for my sour mood continuing to linger. One way or another, she would make my life hell until her father could get over from Moscow and take her off my hands.

The bad mood only worsened when Andre returned with her slung over his shoulder like a sack of potatoes, unconscious again. I swore, and he hurried to defend himself.

"She knocked herself out," he said. "Thrashed around so much she got out of my grip and conked her head on the railing. We should probably use this opportunity to get to the plane, though, don't you think?"

I swore again. He was right. There was no way she'd go of her own accord, and I didn't want her drawing attention to herself. It was imperative no one found out she was with me and where we were heading.

I reached for her, motioning for Andre to grab my suitcase once I had her cradled in my arms. She almost looked sweet and innocent, with her long lashes brushing her cheeks. My loyal bodyguard met me in the hallway only moments later, waiting for instructions.

I groaned, looking toward the emergency exit. "Now we have to use the stairs again instead of taking the elevator like civilized people."

Chapter 5 - Evelina

Once again, I woke up in a strange place, this time with my head pounding. The sound that filled my ears was soothing until I placed it. Was I on a plane?

I sat up, grabbing my throbbing forehead but taking in my surroundings in a couple of pained blinks before I flopped back down from a wave of dizziness. What in hell had that bodyguard done to me? That didn't matter now. Because it was clear I was on my way back to Miami.

Yes, I was on a plane, not just any commercial airline, which certainly wouldn't have allowed Mikhail to carry an unconscious woman. He was powerful, but even his kind of power had its limits.

This was a private jet, and a reasonably large one, with shiny dark wood trim and pale gray upholstery. The window shades were all drawn, but a single lamp cast enough light to see a stainless-steel rolling bar pulled up to the big reclining chair across from the couch I was stretched out on.

Mikhail sprawled on it like it was a throne. His legs wide, and a half-empty glass in one hand, the bottle he'd been obviously pouring from in the other, and his eyes downcast. He'd removed his slim-fitting suit jacket and opened several buttons on his snowy white shirt to reveal tanned skin and a smattering of chest hair beneath it.

Damn it, he looked good. Apparently, sunny Florida agreed with him. I wracked my brain to recall if Kristina had ever mentioned him setting up a base there. None of my cousins ever mentioned it, so at least they weren't at war with each other, which was a relief since he and my father were good friends. If I had known he was based in Miami, I don't think I would have ever wanted to visit so badly. I certainly would have left the second I found out. He noticed I was awake and looked up at me from whatever he'd been musing about in the bottom of his whiskey glass. When did he stop drinking vodka?

Why did I care?

He raised an eyebrow at me but didn't speak. Which was good because I had enough to say for both of us. I pushed aside my mixed-up feelings and concentrated on the burning hot disappointment in my gut. Holding onto my forehead, I flung myself at him, ready to cause enough of a ruckus to bring the plane to an emergency landing if I had to.

"You actually kidnapped me?" I shouted. "And did you let that freak of yours drug me?"

"No one drugged you, Evelina," he said calmly, only stoking my fury.

"Then how was I out long enough for you to get me on this plane? And why does my head hurt so damn much?"

His eyes shot to my forehead, and he stood, taking me by the shoulders and gently but firmly shoving me back onto the couch. He traced his finger along my hairline, and his eyes searched mine, giving me an unwanted shiver. Oh God, he would see through my anger to the truth of how I really felt about him. I shook off his hand and ducked away from the gaze I both craved and feared.

"You knocked yourself out when you tried to get away from Andre," he said, returning to his throne. "I'll keep an eye on you, but I think you'll be fine. Your pupils look normal, and you certainly don't seem weak. Now stay in your seat and enjoy the rest of the flight."

"I'm not a kid," I said. The way his eyes darkened after I said that made me pause, but I couldn't let him ruin everything. "Neither you nor my father have any say about anything in my life anymore."

"We do if it means it might get ended by your own foolishness."

"I can handle myself," I argued, my hands balling into fists when he only snickered at that. I was on his plane, after all. Frustrated tears threatened, but I would have taken a header out of the plane before I let a single one fall. "I'm not going back to Miami. Get your pilot to turn around or land and let me out. You can't make me quit this job I'm doing."

That infuriating eyebrow raised again, along with his fingers, as he answered me. "Yes, you are going back to Miami; no, the plane's not turning around or landing until we get there, and lastly, Evelina?" He paused, but not long enough for me to reply because he wasn't really asking me a question. He rose from his chair and again towered over me, placing a hand on the back of the couch on either side of me, caging me in with his big body. "Yes, I can make you."

He was too close again, making my system go haywire. My eyes drifted shut, and a band of longing squeezed my chest, overriding my crushing disappointment. He was as unyielding as I remembered back when Kristina and I used to try to get away with things. And to think he had been the more lenient of our fathers!

Not even tears would sway him, and I had already decided I'd rather splat on the ground thousands of feet below than let him see me cry. His face was now only inches from mine, and despite the menacing look he was giving me, I forgot why I was so mad. Oh, right, he was trying to control me. I needed to cling to my anger.

God, he was still so sexy. Right then, I didn't care at all that he was being controlling. I wanted nothing more than to feel his lips on mine and for his hands to move an inch to my shoulders and slide their way down my body. He could have done anything to me. Anything! I wanted it all.

But he was still Kristina's father, my own dad's best friend. I couldn't have what I had wanted for half my damn life.

"Fine," I muttered, just so he'd back away and let me breathe again. Or kiss me. That would have been all right, too.

A dozen years of embarrassing fantasies about him flooded my memory as he refused to go back to his seat. I couldn't truthfully say I was disappointed in still being close enough to feel his breath on my cheek or smell his spicy cologne, the same one he always wore. One time during a sleepover at Kristina's, I'd snuck into his room and sprayed it on a tissue. I kept that tissue under my pillow until it dissolved into shreds. I saved my allowance and odd job money for weeks to get him a bottle for Christmas back in eighth grade.

I could call it a crush all I wanted, but I had been in love with this man. To the point it hurt. It would be wise to remember that pain instead of ogling his pecs just inches away. Because he was never going to be mine in the way I wanted. He'd always think of me as his friend's kid who he needed to occasionally pick up from ballet practice—or rescue from a mob hit. I ducked my head and squeezed my eyes shut against the onslaught of memories trying to kill me.

He tipped my chin up. "Look at me," he said, not moving or continuing until I opened my eyes. "A very powerful family wants you dead. I need more than you pretending to agree with me so that I back off. I shouldn't have to remind you that you're my daughter's best friend. I won't sit back and let her be traumatized and heartbroken because you're too stubborn to see reason, let alone stay out of danger." He finally shoved away and returned to his seat but gave me a scathing look that turned my stomach. "Not to mention that you put her in danger by spying from her apartment."

My poor, addled brain did a series of sharp turns. It couldn't have been more than five minutes ago that I wanted to claw his face off for abducting me, and not ten seconds ago, I wanted him to run his hands all over my heated body. Now I was shriveling up with shame as his words sank in. He was right about Kristina, and it never crossed my mind.

"I'm sorry," I said stiffly. "I'd never want Kristina to be hurt."

Just as he knew my agreement from a moment ago hadn't been real, he seemed to sense my apology was sincere, and a genuine smile lit up his face. In a blink, I was forgiven. He took a sip of his drink and held up the glass in a toast.

"Care for a drink? Now that you're all grown up?"

He was teasing me, but mildly and I decided to be good-natured about it. Especially now that his smile had turned a bit mischievous. The twinkle in his eye got me thinking about things I really shouldn't have been thinking about.

"No, thanks," I said.

I had to keep my wits about me. Both to keep from throwing myself at him and to keep an eye out for ways to escape once we touched down. If the Novikoffs hadn't yet figured out that I'd been staying at Kristina's, there might still be a chance to at least get my things back. I had to push aside all thoughts of my thousands of dollars of abandoned computer equipment or risk getting feisty again. I was enjoying his smile far too much at the moment for that.

"Then how about some food?"

When my stomach rumbled at the very mention of something to eat, he jumped up with a grin and went to a curtained-off area. Pulling it aside to reveal a tiny sink and fridge, he began to pull out sandwich fixings.

"We could ask the flight attendant," he said, turning around to give me a look. "But you probably scared her half to death with your accusations."

"True accusations," I reminded him, but my cheeks burned. "I didn't know anyone else was on board."

"Well, they don't fly themselves, and it's regulation to have an attendant. Don't worry; they both work for the organization. In fact, I think your cousin has used both of them in the past."

I nodded. My cousin Ivan had a private jet, but the last time it had set down in Moscow, his brother Yuri had stolen it to come after his runaway bride. I helped locate her, which was how I earned the invitation to Miami in the first place. Still, I was relegated to flying commercial then.

While Mikhail made our meals, I watched in slack-jawed wonder as he sliced the fresh loaf of bread and twisted open a jar of pickles. The way his shirt pulled against his muscles and his firm, sure hands wielded the bread knife held me in thrall until he turned around again. I quickly pretended to study my long-neglected fingernails.

He handed me a plate with a fat turkey and cheese sandwich, a pickle slice, and apple wedges on the side. I almost waited for him to hand me a juice box with the straw already in it, but he plopped a water bottle down instead. I had to stop feeling childish around him. It was driving me nuts, especially since I couldn't stop ogling him.

"So, it's been a long time," he said, once again sitting across from me so I had the full glorious view every time he lifted a bite to his lips.

"About two years," I agreed.

Not long enough. Since I had stopped having dreams about him, I thought I was over my infatuation, but it was back like it never left. The only way I could truly get over him was to cut all ties with Kristina, so I was never faced with his picture or had to hear his name, then force myself into a relationship with an appropriate man my age. Those options were abhorrent to me, especially cutting off my oldest and dearest friend.

He asked me what I'd been up to and seemed to be eagerly awaiting my response. I couldn't tell him about my current project because he'd ruined it, putting me back in a bad mood. So, I updated him about my investigation firm in Moscow, Leo's most recent facial recognition program, and then we gossiped about people we both knew. He didn't bring Kristina up again, or my father and I followed suit. It was almost like I wanted to be there, not conked over the head and dragged aboard.

"Tell me what you've been doing," I urged, sandwiches long finished.

I could feel the plane slowly dropping altitude and didn't want to face the unknown yet. As soon as the plane landed, I'd have to be on the lookout for escape options, and right then… I didn't really want to escape.

A dark cloud seemed to pass over his face, his eyes shuttering. "Things are good," he said slowly.

"Oh yeah, I can tell by your face that things are thriving."

He shouted with laughter and shook his head. "It's just the same old thing. Fighting for power, gaining power, having to fight someone new for it all over again."

I was stunned. Was he actually letting me into his deepest thoughts? Treating me like an adult?

"Rough time lately?" I asked, fighting the urge to move to his side and take his hand.

"Really rough time," he said. The flight attendant stuck her head through a door near the front of the cabin and told us we should buckle up for landing. I frowned at her, wanting to share more with Mikhail. But he only gave me an arch look as he reached for his seatbelt. "I was supposed to be on vacation, you know."

He wasn't really chastening me, or I would have let him have it again. He was joking around like he might have with any friend. Still treating me like an adult and not a wayward child.

I really liked it. If he could see me as an adult—a peer and not someone he was responsible for—that opened up a world of possibilities. A bunch of those delicious possibilities passed through my mind in a rush, and I snuck a glance at him while I buckled my safety belt. He looked straight at me in a way I couldn't quite place, certainly unlike any look he'd ever given me before. Wait a second.

Was he thinking of the possibilities as well?

I nearly cracked myself up at that. Of course, he wasn't because he didn't see me as an adult. He was probably appeasing me, like a child, to keep me from having a tantrum. Which I had basically done. Like a child. I scowled, and he rolled his eyes and looked away.

The plane landed a few minutes later with a mild thump, and I gathered my anger around me to defuse the last traces of lust Mikhail had once again drawn forward. It needed to stay stuffed down because I had been days, hours, maybe only minutes from a breakthrough in bringing the Novikoffs to their knees. And Mikhail had wrecked that, left behind all my equipment, and was going to keep me locked up who-knew-where until my Papa collected me like I got lost in a shopping center.

But not if I escaped first.

Oh, I tried really hard to stay pissed off, but then I caught him looking at me again. And I started thinking again about the possibilities. Maybe I could get him out of my system once and for all? If I had to spend the foreseeable future cooped up with him, surely I could get something out of it to ease my disappointment.

The fuse had been sparked, and I didn't know how long it would burn before it exploded.

Chapter 6 - Mikhail

She was going to kill me. I was positive of it. I'd almost forgotten her fiery nature, and her heated response to finding out she was in the air and on her way back to Miami would have amused me if it didn't turn me on so damn much. Combined with her curves, her little outburst only fanned the flames of the desire I was trying my hardest to douse.

Once I all but shoved her back onto the couch, she still looked up at me with rage burning in her eyes. Still, underneath it, there was a deep disappointment I would have done anything to assuage. I wasn't trying to destroy her dreams, damn it. I was trying to keep her safe. But she was having none of it.

She flat-out refused to accept she was in danger, only focused on her goal. Admirable if she didn't have a price on her head.

It took all my willpower not to wrap my fingers in her lustrous hair and yank her head back so her pouting lips would be easier to claim. It would have been a very nice way to shut her up. Then she had the absolute gall to shrug me off and pretend to agree with me. As if I hadn't seen that gambit before, hundreds of times, from both Evelina and Kristina. Infuriating.

She wasn't selfish, and when I brought up the possible danger she'd put her best friend in, she instantly became contrite. It was clear she was sincerely sorry, going pale at the thought of Kristina being in danger, and all my anger evaporated. Just like it did when they learned their lesson back in the day. Within minutes we were on easy terms again, and I was making her a sandwich, just like the old days.

God, I wished I could stop thinking of my daughter and Evelina's history together, forget the past between us and just see her as the sexy, vibrant woman she was today. I'd love to tell her how impressed I was that she'd managed to infiltrate one of the most powerful families in New York, but I had to stay stern. Had to keep that boundary.

As I watched her enjoy her meal, her tongue darting out to lick away a crumb, I began to wonder why I was so intent on keeping her distant. Why was that tongue not trailing down my chest and lower... She was a gorgeous, fiercely independent, intelligent, and ambitious woman. She'd be someone I'd be seriously interested in if I'd just met her.

That was where the trouble lay. I didn't just meet her; I'd known her since she was ten. Because she was my daughter's best friend. And the killing blow I needed to lay to rest my wayward lust—she was my best friend's daughter. Not just any old pal but a powerful entity in his own right. If I so much as placed a finger on Evelina's curvy ass, I'd be the one with a hit out on me.

So, yeah, I had to stop thinking about her ass. I was here to protect her, nothing more.

That didn't mean either of us had to be completely miserable, so I kept things light, having her fill me in on her successful business back in Moscow. It seemed like she had come around until the plane started its final descent, then she became sullen and stubborn again. Well, it was a peaceful few hours, anyway.

My driver was waiting for me on the tarmac of the private airfield, along with another bodyguard who'd be following us in a separate car. So far, I was sure no one other than Oleg knew I was involved, but it was always better to err on the side of caution. I'd had my share of double crosses in the past and had learned the hard way.

Evelina was as docile as a lamb as we made our way down the steps and across the lot, not even nagging me about where we were going from here. I hoped her spirit wasn't completely broken at the same time as I was glad I didn't have to haul her over my shoulder and forcefully stuff her in the backseat.

I reached over to open the car door for her, and when I straightened up, she was running full out across the empty airfield toward the highway. Which was separated from the airport by a ten-foot-high fence topped with razor wire.

With a sigh, I waved away the bodyguard and took off after her. Where in blazes did she think she was going? If she somehow scaled the fence before I caught up with her, what would she do next? Hitch a ride somewhere? Call a cab? I had her phone and her wallet. She was as good as mine.

That thought hit me so hard that I nearly stopped running after her. No, she could never be mine. I put on a burst of speed to rid myself of any ideas of possessing Evelina, no matter how intriguing they were, and easily caught up to her.

Wrapping my hand around her upper arm, I dragged her back. She was too out of breath to do much until we were back at the car, but before I could cram her in and get the hell out of there, she promptly went off on me. Again.

She hit me twice in the shoulder in rapid succession, and I swore at the ruthless stab of pain that rocketed down my arm. I'd injured that shoulder long ago, and it still gave me trouble sometimes, and that little brat knew it. I really didn't want to get rough with her, but she was out of control, aiming for my face with her fists now.

"I'm back in Miami now, so just let me go and butt out," she shouted as she landed a solid blow on the side of my head. "I don't need you, Mikhail!"

That hurt worse than the cracks to the shoulder. And it pissed me off enough to stop standing there like a heavy bag at the gym. I grabbed her flailing hands and held them behind her back. She seemed stunned that I immobilized her so quickly, forgetting how well I knew her fighting style.

"Don't you understand they'll expect you to go to one of your cousins' houses?" I shouted right back at her. "They'll be watching and waiting, and yes, the Morozovs have a lot of power, but the Novikoffs are pissed. And they don't hold grudges, Evelina. Because once they set their sights on someone, that person doesn't stay alive long enough to warrant one."

"I can take care of myself," she yelled, trying to jerk free.

Enough was enough. I slammed her against the side of the car, pinning her there with my body.

Bad idea. Every soft curve was molded to me, and every angry, gasping breath she took as she berated me made her breasts heave against my chest and made my cock go as stiff as an iron pole. She went still, and suddenly the way she looked at me wasn't filled with the fury of a thousand suns. It was just as hot, though. Intent, like she wanted something from me. Something I'd love to give but couldn't. I let go of her hands and tangled my fingers in her hair.

It was as soft and silky as I'd imagined since she was on my hotel room bed. Her eyes flared, and her chest rose, her nipples brushing against my chest and making me swell enough to almost lose control. Almost. I couldn't have her looking at me like that, couldn't let her part her lips and sigh as she leaned into me.

I had to wipe that glimmer of desire from her eyes before I gave her exactly what she seemed to want from me.

"God damn it, Evelina," I hissed, gripping her hair tighter and forcing everything I was feeling to come out as anger.

This girl needed to be scared of me and quit fooling around.

CHAPTER 7 - EVELINA

The anger blazing from his eyes, so dark now that they looked black, didn't fool me one bit. Every inch of what he was really feeling was pressed against my belly, and I liked it. I knew I wasn't misreading those strange looks he'd given me on the plane, and I felt vindicated. And, more importantly, emboldened.

This was my chance to make up for my disappointment, at least a little bit. Who was I fooling? A lot. Every thought in my mind was centered on his thick bulge pushed against me, his fingers tangled in my hair.

"God damn it, Evelina," he growled, spitting mad at my last-ditch attempt at freedom.

In truth, I had no plan; just needed to give it my all, like I did with everything. Like I was about to do now. He thought I was going to cower at his tone, his fierce scowl? Oh, sure, he was brutal, but he must have forgotten how well I knew him. He would never, ever raise his hand to a woman.

And when his eyes dropped to my lips, I knew he wouldn't turn me over to his bodyguard, either. I was all his, and the possibilities unleashed in my imagination made me go a little wild.

I forced my back away from the car, even though he had me firmly pinned with his big body and ground against the steel pressing against my core. He hissed out a swear word but ducked his head closer. I could feel his hot breath on my cheek, and my neck tingled where his hand lay.

Even as he tightened his grip on my hair, shivers of desire coursed through me.

His free hand raised. Where would it land? On my cheek? My hip? God, my breast? I licked my lips, straining against him.

"What, Mikhail?" I asked. My voice came out low and harsh.

His driver and bodyguard were only a few yards away, but they might as well have been in another country for all I cared. Mikhail's body was pressed against mine, his lips close enough to kiss me until I melted. I was already close to melting, my panties soaked from all the fantasies I'd ever had about him so close to coming true.

He lifted his gaze from my mouth, and his brows drew together over eyes that seemed to be confused now. I almost laughed. To think he'd set out to scare me into submission. Didn't he know I didn't have to be scared to do whatever he wanted?

Raising my hands to his chest, I gently curled my fingers in the crisp fabric of his shirt. "What?" I repeated.

Tell me what you want. Better yet, throw me into the backseat and show me!

For a split second, I couldn't breathe. It looked like he might do what I was silently begging for. He jerked his hand out of my hair and dragged me aside so he could open the door. The next second I was tossed like a ragdoll into the backseat, but the door slammed before I could reach for him. I was alone. The sudden loss of his heat and hard muscles—hard everything—took my breath away. It took me several breaths to realize he was storming away from the car.

"Take her to the compound," he shouted as he passed the driver.

I scrambled to open the door and either try another escape attempt or jump into his arms; I really wasn't sure. But he turned on his heel and yanked it open, sticking his head in.

"I'm going to be in the car right behind you the whole way. Don't try jumping out at a stop light because I'll be right on top of you before you can blink."

I nearly bellowed that that was what I wanted. For him to be on top of me. He slammed the door again, and the driver got in, giving me a sheepish look in the rearview mirror. He looked resigned to having a miserable time, but no one's misery could have rivaled mine.

Nothing. I had nothing. No control over my future. My project was left in the dust and destined to be considered a failure by my father.

Worst of all, Mikhail had fought his evident desire and won. I felt how much he wanted me. Felt every inch of how much. I shifted in my seat with a long groan.

"Are you too hot?" the driver asked, handing a bottle of water to me over the seat.

Yes. Yes, I was. But not from being back in the Florida weather. I took the bottle with a sour look, and after that, he raised the partition between us.

Taking a long swig, I settled in to stew about my situation. I had no idea where we were going, but it looked like we were heading south. I felt naked without my phone, wishing I could pull up a map and have a satellite tell me where I was. There was nothing but the quickly moving scenery outside to distract me. However, that far south in Florida mainly was water or trees and not much else. Try as I might, I kept returning to the fact that Mikhail might be feeling the same way about me as I felt about him.

Okay, certainly not the same way. I'd been pining over him since I first met him. The world's hottest dad. That short time on the plane, when he treated me like an equal, had been amazing and had made me see why I still had feelings for him. Even though he might not have that lengthy history of wanting the hell out of me like I did for him, he wanted me. At that moment, yes, he did. I felt the evidence. And that shook me to the core.

I lost out on something I wanted, but maybe I could get something else in whatever time I had with Mikhail. If he didn't just dump me at this mysterious compound, he mentioned with his bodyguards.

That thought brought back my bitterness about my Novikoff project. Being as close as I was and having it stolen from me was a tough pill to swallow. Not to mention my expensive equipment, all my data, and the proprietary software that Leo created. Mikhail had left it behind like it was garbage and not my life's work.

I didn't like simmering with anger, but it was better than simmering with lust. Even if I could finally get what I longed for from Mikahil, I was still shit out of luck as far as proving myself as a leader. And that was his fault. I needed to remember that. I refused to let his gorgeous face, his dreamy smile, and his hard, hard body distract me from that.

Wherever we went, I'd just have to find a way to escape before my father arrived.

We kept driving interminably, heading further and further out into the jungles of the Everglades. With every passing mile, the roads grew narrower and more deserted, and my chances of escape grew slimmer. I kept my eyes peeled as we turned onto what looked like no more than a poorly beaten track. Soon, the car was swallowed up by palmetto bushes and towering cypresses and oaks with Spanish moss hanging in long ropes that eerily brushed the side windows as we inched along.

Now I was feeling the first inklings of fear. Not even a seasoned hunter loaded up with weapons would survive very long out here. Maybe this was a shortcut to a nice resort on one of the Keys?

I perked up a little as we bumped along over a series of bridges but deflated again when we pulled up at a gate that might have been designed after a medieval castle's defense system. The driver got out, walked up to a screen outside the brick and iron monstrosity, and began speaking. I turned around to see the car following us pull up behind us, and Mikhail got out as well.

My heart fluttered at the same time my stomach dropped. Pressing my face to the window like a puppy who missed its master, I tried to catch his eye as he headed back to the other car, but he resolutely ignored me. Hmmph, so it was going to be like that, was it?

The gate finally opened, and the driver pulled past the six-foot thick wall. My stomach rolled over again when I watched it slide shut as soon as Mikhail's car was through. I'd need climbing tools or a ladder to get over the twelve-foot high wall, wire cutters to get through the razor wire at the top, and I was pretty certain the whole kit and caboodle were electrified up there, so I'd have to find out where the main circuit breaker was before I did anything else.

After going over another bridge, we turned onto a wider road through more dense foliage before it opened up into a vast clearing, paved with white crushed shells and dotted with rose and hibiscus bushes. I gaped at the building in the center of the clearing, like a massive jewel set in platinum.

It was styled like a Spanish hacienda, with three stories sprawled nearly to the edges of our island. The pink and cream stucco against the almost violently blue sky made me feel like I'd been dropped into a fairy tale. Expansive balconies lined the front, all loaded with flowering plants and potted fruit trees, and a sweeping staircase led up to the porch, where double doors stood under towering pillars wrapped with vines.

The vines snapped me out of my awe. The place was a palace, but one on a secluded island in the middle of the Everglades, surrounded by water that was rife with alligators and an overgrown, swampy jungle that was riddled with snakes, among all the other wild beasts I couldn't name. The last ounce of my hope dissolved away. I was a city girl from Moscow. The heat alone would kill me before the critters ever got a chance. I'd be an easy meal for them.

Before I could sink into despair, I reminded myself of who I was and what I was made of. This was only the front of the place, and I refused to give up before I explored every option. I didn't give up just because things were rough. I could still get my goals back on track. It was probably for the best that Mikhail was going to give me the cold shoulder, so I wouldn't be distracted.

To my surprise, he opened the car door for me with a conciliatory smile. I began to soften, forget about the fact I was basically his prisoner, and felt my damn fool face start to smile back. Hell no.

I swept past him toward the steps, keeping my eyes forward when he caught up to me and opened the door. I pretended not to be impressed even as I subtly gaped at the luxurious interior. Besides the marble floors and richly papered walls, there were bamboo ceiling fans slowly twirling above, interspersed with crystal chandeliers. The furniture was a bizarre mix of casual rattan with bright floral cushions and items that might have come from 17th-century Versailles. It somehow worked, though.

He led me to a room on the second floor and pushed open the door for me, motioning for me to go in. I took a step inside and couldn't help gasping. Did I truly step into a fairy tale? Because of my line of work and family upbringing, I'd never been much of a girly girl—at least outwardly. But all the plush white pillows piled onto the icy blue bedspread, the giant, antique canopy bed with sheer lace hanging across the top and billowing down the sides, the gilt mirror over the delicate vanity table that held a silver vase full of pink roses had me hooked.

Much nicer than my serviceable place back home and miles more luxurious than Kristina's comfy Brooklyn apartment. It even made my cousin's fabulous mansions look rather plain.

"I'm glad you like it," he said, reading my face. I struggled to work up a scowl as I ignored him. With a sigh, he took my chin in his hand and forced me to look at him. I very nearly let go of my resolve to escape. "Try to view this as a vacation," he said, giving me a smile that had me weak in the knees. "Maybe you'll have a little fun until the all-clear is called."

Oh God, my resolve was pretty much gone. Why not? Why not have some fun if he'd only let go of his own stupid resolve and have some with me. But he wouldn't, and I did have some pride. I gave him a look I hoped would sear his skin off and slammed into the room.

Chapter 8 - Mikhail

After Evelina slammed the door in my face, I didn't expect to see her for the rest of her time here. Which should have been for the best, so I wasn't sure why I was so disappointed in the sudden chilly attitude.

Not after she had practically devoured me with her eyes and rubbed that soft, curvy body of hers against me. I never should have gotten so close, and the feel of her was still very much alive in my thoughts. How did I lose control like that?

Because she was irresistible, that's how I had to resist her. So, it was for the best that she was going to pout and hide herself away from me. I needed to get my mind off of her and shut myself up in my study, text Kristina, and tell her to call me back as soon as she could. Fortunately, Evelina had told me on the plane that my daughter was out of town, but I needed to keep her from returning home, all while not scaring her half to death.

She thought she was safe from our life because she distanced herself from me. Still, the truth was, she was never going to be completely safe as long as she insisted on living by herself, outside of my immediate protection. Sometimes it killed me to let her have the independence she craved, and I counted the hours until she grew bored of trying to become a movie star. It had already been going on far too long without the breakthrough she thought would happen as soon as she stepped foot on American soil.

I admired her fortitude and believed she had talent. I also understood reality and how very few people made it in the acting game, and yes, I wanted her to come back under my wing until she was married to someone I approved of and who would cherish her as I did.

I snickered at myself as I headed out onto the back deck to pour myself a much-needed drink and wait for her reply. Both Kristina and Evelina would tear into me if they could hear my old-fashioned thoughts. One day they'd understand when they had children of their own.

The thought of Evelina having children with some unknown man gave me a pang I didn't want to explore, and thankfully, Kristina returned my message before I could really get upset by such an idea. Why would I have any right to get upset?

I'm in Connecticut doing a TV show; isn't that great! They gave me more lines too, and I might get a storyline if fans like my character.

That's wonderful. I texted back, pretending I hadn't grilled Evelina about her already. I wished she would just call me so I could hear her voice and assure myself she was all right, but there was no reason to panic her. Yet. I frowned as I continued to type. *Remember the acting workshop you told me about? It sounds like a solid investment, so I went ahead and signed you up.*

Her reply was almost instantaneous. *Oh my God, thank you! I can't believe it!*

I grumbled, not liking that she thought I was coming around to agreeing with her choices. *But you have to go to LA as soon as you wrap. Don't go back to NY.*

Sure. But Evelina's staying with me. Is she okay?

Ah, she knew something was wrong without me having to say it. She would always have ties to the Bratva whether she wanted to or not. But how did I answer this last question without saying something was wrong? I remembered I had confiscated Evelina's phone and went to find it. I probably could have had one of my security guys crack the lock screen code for me, but that might take a while, and I didn't want Kristina to worry. As I headed upstairs, my daughter's message flashed across the screen.

I knocked on the door, and when Evelina opened it, I held the phone out. Her eyes widened with gratitude, nearly breaking my heart. As if I'd give her phone back.

"Tell Kristina you got a job and had to leave New York," I said brusquely.

46

We stared at each other for a few seconds until she finally snatched it from my hand, tapping furiously at the screen. She turned away, but I gripped her shoulder and turned her back around, holding my palm open for the phone.

"No one can know you're here," I said. "Not even Leo. For his own safety," I added.

"Fine," she muttered, then her shoulders slumped. "Look, I get it, okay? I won't call or text anyone. But if I have my phone, I might be able to get back online with the Novikoff's cameras."

That made me laugh, which made her scowl. "Then you're really not getting it back," I told her.

She seemed to understand how serious I was. She begrudgingly handed it over, and I kept my finger on the screen before she could turn it off and keep it from locking again. Before I even turned away, she slammed the door on me, but I was already walking back downstairs and scrolling through her messages to make sure she hadn't compromised our position.

It turned out she'd only done what I asked her and let Kristina know she'd be leaving her apartment for a while. Kristina's answer was filled with excitement about the extremely expensive workshop I was going to have to sign her up for, along with finding her suitable accommodations in Los Angeles. As much as I didn't want to encourage her pipe dream, she'd be safer out there.

I didn't really have time to keep running through Evelina's messages, but for some reason, curiosity made me keep scrolling. There wasn't much between her and Kristina, just benign plans and lots of silly memes. The messages between her and her brother were full of computer jargon and more memes.

I shook my head as I looked through her contacts and then back to her messages. Was there a boyfriend? There were plenty of male names but few messages, and they were short and to the point, anything but romantic.

Disgusted with myself, I turned off her phone and locked it in my desk drawer. I was here to protect her, not spy on her. And why did it matter if she had a boyfriend or not? It was of no consequence at all.

After I coerced the acting clinic into accepting Kristina at such short notice by paying an exorbitant fee, I found her a place to stay with a family who used to work for me back in Moscow. They retired to sunny California a few years back and still helped me on the odd occasion. The most important thing was that I trusted them, and they understood the seriousness of the situation, promising to keep a watchful eye on anything out of the ordinary while she was there.

I barely got my drink out on the deck when the cook called that dinner was ready. Thinking that Evelina would stay upstairs, I instructed her to put together a tray and take it up to her.

"The young lady is already in the dining room," she answered.

Surprised that she was going to grace me with her presence, I hustled to meet her, my mood getting lighter with every step down the long hallway. I hadn't been to my Everglades fortress in a long time, and it would have been a shame to waste the grand place, so I was glad she had decided to lighten up. I was also glad to get a chance to talk to her some more since I'd enjoyed the small amount of time on the plane that she wasn't trying to kill me.

My mood soured the second I entered the dining room. Evelina stood on one side of the long, walnut table, leaning across the wide surface to reach a covered serving dish. I stopped dead and could only stare. She was no longer wearing the tight jeans and body-hugging t-shirt but had changed into a dress that might have been painted on and was so short I could almost see the rounded tops of her perfect ass peeking out beneath the clingy black fabric. It had a strap tied around her neck, leaving her shoulders and arms bare, and the top dipped so low her ripe breasts were millimeters from bouncing free as she pulled the tray closer and sat down.

Once her backside was hidden from view, I could breathe again, but my cock had sprung back to life and refused to back down. Not with that almost sheer fabric molding to every last inch of her. Dear God, was she not wearing a bra? She was going to kill me.

Actually, I realized her skimpy dress was probably my fault. While I waited for her to wake up in the New York hotel, I'd called one of my guys and told him I'd be having a woman staying with me here and to make sure she had clothes when we arrived. He promised he'd have his girlfriend go shopping right away, but she must have thought I meant a romantic rendezvous, not a hostage situation with my best friend's daughter.

Evelina certainly did look good. Too good. As much as I liked looking at her in a dress like that, it was close to torture not being able to touch. And how I wanted to touch her. My hands balled into fists as I fought the urge to bend her over the table again, this time with me behind her, sliding that dress up over her hips and yanking whatever panties she had on down her smooth thighs. That is, if she was wearing any.

I groaned, making her realize I was standing in the doorway. Our eyes locked for a second before she quickly turned away. There was no possible way she didn't read the intention in my stare.

I had to get it together, or I'd not only be fucking Evelina on the dining room table but fucking up any chance I had of living much longer afterward. Friendship only went so far, and Oleg wouldn't rest until I was obliterated off the face of the earth for despoiling his little girl.

Who was anything but a little girl anymore, not with the way she was smiling at me. So, she'd chosen to make things pleasant between us? It would have been better to ignore her, grab a plate, and leave. Hell, I wasn't thinking about food at all—but I chose to prolong the torture.

"Glad you decided to join me," I said, sitting across from her.

It served the purpose of being out of reach of grabbing her, but now I had a full view of her voluptuous breasts.

Since she was anything but stupid, she noticed exactly where my gaze fell and took a deep breath before answering with a knowing grin on her pretty face.

"Oh well, I decided you were right," she purred. "About treating this like a vacation and maybe having a little fun."

A dozen different ways I would have liked to have fun with her raced through my mind. Her eyes sparkled as if she could read my thoughts. Was she toying with me? If so, it was a dangerous game, one I couldn't let her win. I slapped my hand down on the table, making her jump. And bounce. Swearing up a storm, I reached for the green salad and loaded up my plate.

"Knock it off," I ordered.

Her eyes flew wide. "Knock what off?"

"You're trying to get something from me." I didn't want a war, so I leaned back and sighed. "I thought we'd gotten past that on the plane."

Her face screwed up, her cheeks red, letting me know I was right. She didn't answer me, and I concentrated on eating, all while staring resolutely at my plate. But every time she reached for something, she had to stand up slightly, being so petite while the table was so large. Every time, my glance flew to those lush mounds threatening to tip out of her dress, all but begging me to cup them. Draw those pert nipples into my mouth. God damn it.

I ate at lightning speed, certain by the time she reached for the water pitcher for the third time and kept replacing it far from her that she knew exactly what she was doing. She wanted me to stare at her tits, wanted to arouse me. Yes, it was working, and it was also pissing me off.

She was beginning to wear me down. The way she'd responded after trying to run from the airport, grinding against me with a challenge in her eyes, the way she looked now. It was getting to be too much, and I was about to lean across the table and take a handful of what she'd been offering during the entire tense meal.

Instead, I stood up abruptly, turning before she could see my cock about to tear through my pants.

"What's wrong?" she asked, sounding genuinely confused.

"I have things to do," I snapped.

"I thought you were supposed to be on vacation?" she challenged.

Damn it, did she want me to tear her dress off her and take her six different ways before we even made it upstairs?

What if she did?

That thought was much too intriguing—and dangerous—to consider for long.

"That all changed when you decided to meddle in things over your head. Then get a price on it." I waited at the door through her beat of silence.

"Mikhail, wait," she finally said, voice beseeching. I turned and waited. Not sure what I wanted her to say or what I wanted to hear. "Can I please have my phone back? I understand nobody can know I'm here. I promise not to call or text anyone. I know I'm only here for my own good."

To think I'd already been tossing around the idea of giving it back. I could cut the internet access in the house, and she couldn't get in too much trouble with it then, could she? If only I didn't believe a word out of the very same mouth, I wanted to kiss until she was breathless. I had to get out before I really lost control.

"Not on your life," I snapped, storming out of the room and freeing myself from her spell.

CHAPTER 9 - EVELINA

I watched him stomp out of the dining room that was fit for royalty and leaned back in my chair. Crossing my arms over my chest, I could only scowl in defeat at the food left on the table. I didn't get my phone back, and he still refused to be seduced. Didn't he find me attractive in this insanely sleazy dress?

When I first saw how nice my room was, it went a long way to ease my bad mood. As upset as I was over losing my computer setup and all my hard work, there wasn't anything I could do about it. Being pissed off only wasted the energy I needed to formulate a plan. It was best to find a bright side, as my brother Leo would have told me.

I wasn't in danger of getting murdered by the Novikoffs. That was a certain bright side. And this was one of the most amazing places I'd ever stayed. I decided to explore the enormous suite. The bathroom didn't disappoint with its giant claw foot tub, waterfall shower the size of my kitchen back in Moscow, and the thickest, softest towels I'd ever felt. High-end skincare products were at the dainty little vanity table, and a plush robe was hanging outside the walk-in closet door.

I almost forgot I wasn't there of my own volition until I opened the closet doors. Dozens of slinky dresses hung on one side, each one racier than the next. Sexy, barely there lingerie was neatly folded in the center drawer console. Mile-high, strappy heels—fuck me heels, if ever any existed, lined the baseboard beneath the dresses. Casual wear? Sure. Booty shorts, halters that might have doubled as bikini tops, and, oh yes, actual bikinis.

It might have looked trashy, but I recognized expensive designer names on all the labels. A luxurious wardrobe designed to entice, but whose was it? Of course, they had to belong to his girlfriend.

It made me almost double over at the thought of Mikhail using this place as some sort of love nest. The idea of his woman wearing these outfits for him, and worse, him liking it, made me want to throw up. The overwhelming jealousy was ridiculous and turned my anger back onto myself.

Here I thought I had finally moved on from the crush on Mikhail that kept me from exploring genuine, meaningful relationships with guys my age. Was I destined to die single because none of them ever lived up to him? Not in looks, accomplishments, or character. He was the one I wanted, no one else. It was a relief when he left Moscow, even though it tore me to shreds not to be able to see him regularly and feed my hopeless dreams that one day we'd be together.

Of course, Kristina reminded me of him, and my feelings would be rekindled whenever I visited her, but the more time went by, the easier it was to bury them again. Now that I had to be stuck in the same house with him? Now that I knew he must feel something for me, even if it was only simple lust? Torture. Pure torture. Especially imagining what kind of sophisticated, worldly woman was wearing those clothes for him.

I really didn't want to wear any of those outfits, but after a long, hot shower, I didn't want to put on the grubby clothes I'd been kidnapped in, either. I picked out one of the more demure dresses, which was still anything but, and went downstairs when the cook urged me to try the meal she made. I was determined not to let him have any effect on me.

Yeah, that went well.

I picked at the remains of my dinner, which was a truly delicious blackened chicken with Cuban seasonings, reminded of how he looked when he appeared in the dining room doorway.

He was more handsome and sexy in faded jeans and a close-fitting t-shirt than in his tailored suit. The effect was immediate, but then he looked shocked and appalled at what I was wearing, probably comparing it to what it looked like on his girlfriend. Maybe wondering how I had the nerve to wear it in the first place? It wasn't like I wanted to wear his stripper girlfriend's clothes and be spilling out all over the place, and he should have shown me where the washer and dryer was if he wanted me to wear my own things.

He kept giving me those horrified looks the entire meal like he wanted to reach across the table and smack me. On top of that, he still refused to give me my phone back even when I told him I knew I was there for my well-being. It wouldn't do any good to message my brother if he thought I was safest with Mikhail. For all I knew, my father was already coming to pick me up and drag me back to Russia.

My only chance was to access my secret backup files stored on the cloud. Then maybe I could salvage my project. But no. He was immovable. I was stuck with no chance of accessing my data and getting things back on track.

I finally left the dining room but was too wound up to be close to sleepy, and there was no TV or any books in my suite. This place was almost as big as a shopping mall, so I decided to explore. So what if Mikhail didn't like it? What was he going to do? Scold me like the child he still thought I was and send me to my room?

The first half of the downstairs area was mostly locked doors and the big, modern kitchen. I offered to help the cook with the dishes, but she only laughed and told me where the media room was upstairs. It was just where she described, and I walked around the ceiling-high bookshelves, marveling at the selection. There was everything from illustrated fairy tales to weighty philosophy tomes. Overstuffed armchairs and couches beckoned for me to curl up in one with one of the books, but I was still too wired to concentrate. A big tv took up the better part of the opposite wall, with a recessed seating area and a fridge stocked with cold drinks and fresh fruit.

"This room is bigger than my apartment," I said, almost expecting an echo.

Opening the curtains revealed a balcony, and I noticed I was looking out at the back of the house now. I pulled open the sliding door and stepped outside, getting hit in the face with a wall of humidity. No wonder everything was so green around here; all the plants got plenty of water. Making my way along the balcony, I turned a corner and saw a swimming pool tucked away in a grotto. Just a few minutes outside, I was sweating through my dress, and the azure water called me to jump in.

The scene became more inviting when a splash drew my eye to a spot between several palms obscuring half the pool. I leaned over the balcony to see Mikhail doing laps. Like a cartoon character, my eyes popped out of my head to see his back and arm muscles rippling as he sliced through the water. He flipped over to do the backstroke for a length of the pool, and I went into a trance at the sight of his taut six-pack and sculpted pecs.

How was this man forty-four years old?

My breathing hitched as I leaned far enough to tumble into the potted plants and the brick walkway below. There were no more thoughts about my backup data and certainly no more thoughts of escaping. I only wanted to watch Mikhail cut through the water with powerful strokes. I wasn't even mad anymore, just… entranced. That was what he always did to me.

I suddenly decided a dip in the pool was the only thing that would get my nervous energy out. I simply wouldn't be able to get to sleep without a refreshing swim. Racing back to my room, I found the selection of bathing suits, frowning at the thought of his girlfriend as I pulled on a red string bikini. It was foolish to despise a woman I'd never met just because she might have worn it before me. Foolish to hate her because Mikhail might have looked at her wearing it and been aroused.

What if I could make him forget all about her?

It wasn't outside the realm of possibility, not after what I'd felt pressing against me at the airfield. With my thoughts as jumbled as ping pong balls set free in a hurricane, I raced down the stairs and searched for a door that would lead to the pool.

He was just getting out when I found the path that led to the grotto, and I paused on the stepping stones to stare at him. He shook his head, sending water droplets flying from his tousled hair, finally noticing me standing there. His eyes widened as he took me in, almost every inch of me since I was wearing that scandalous swimsuit without a coverup over it. He licked his lips as if he wanted to taste me, and I shivered, emboldened by how much I wanted to be close to him.

Grabbing a towel from a rack, I quickly handed it to him. But once I was within touching range, I couldn't stop myself and began to dry his chest for him. He seemed frozen, and our eyes locked. The feel of his hard chest under my hands made me step a little closer, moving the towel over his shoulders.

"How many laps did you do?" I asked. My mind raced, and I forced a teasing tone to my voice. "Do you think you could do a few more to keep me company?" I braced myself for the blow of his rejection.

Instead, he took the towel from me and lightly whacked me on the behind with it. "You never were a very good swimmer," he teased right back.

I both loved and hated that he knew me so well. But at least he was getting back into the pool. I hurried down the steps from the shallow end with him, and we both eased beneath the cool water at the same time. I dipped my head back to soak my hair and turned in a circle with my fingers spread wide, sighing contentedly at how refreshing it felt to my heated skin.

I stopped turning to see him scowling at me. What did I do now to earn that look? My first instinct was to strike out before he did. Still, my feelings were in such a tangle. I really only wanted a peaceful evening. That is, if he wasn't going to ravage me the way I wanted. Peace was my second choice.

I splashed him and jogged toward the deep end before he could retaliate. He caught up with me in two strokes and cut his hand through the water, sending a veritable tsunami at me. I flopped onto my back and kicked water at him as I spluttered and paddled to get away.

Soon we were chasing each other back and forth and laughing harder than I'd laughed in a long time. I pretended to call a truce, and as soon as he was close enough, I let him have it with a big swish of my entire arm, soaking him and making him lunge for me. With a shriek, I kicked off the bottom and headed for the deep end, with him shouting he was going to make me pay.

I turned as I chugged toward the opposite side, ready to tell him he'd never catch me when my foot slipped as the bottom dipped downward. The next thing I knew, I was slipping under. I wasn't really a lousy swimmer and could have found my footing and pushed my head above water, but his strong arms immediately wrapped around me and pulled me up, dragging me to the edge.

I had never once acted like a damsel in distress to get what I wanted, and though I had wanted Mikhail for years, I still wasn't about to start. I took what I wanted, even if it got me in trouble. Before he could let me go, I wrapped my arms around his neck and held on, his face close enough to mine to kiss him, our bodies pressed together under the gently swishing water. He stared at me as if mesmerized, his eyes finally dropped to my breasts, pushed close to his chest, and billowed out of the tiny top. He looked back up at me, at my mouth. I closed my eyes, waiting to feel his lips on mine, my whole body yearning for it.

Instead, he lifted me up onto the side of the pool and backed away. "I can't do this," he said raggedly.

But he wanted to. I reached out with my feet and drew him back between my legs, crossing my ankles behind his shoulders.

"Yes, you can," I said. *Please*, I was inwardly begging.

His hands broke the surface and slid along my calves and up my thighs to rest on my hips. It was almost as if I could see his fight with himself. But why? I tightened my legs, pulling him closer. Close enough, he could take my bikini bottoms off with his teeth. He planted his hands on the smooth cement on either side of me and pulled himself effortlessly out of the deep water. Drops rained down on me as his body pressed against mine, forcing me to lean back. I shook with anticipation and need.

"No, I can't." He shoved away from me, back into the water. He swam to the other side and climbed out, stamping away down the path without looking at me again.

I wanted to yell at him that he was a coward, the worst insult I could fling at him. But I knew he was only being noble. In his mind, he had a job to do. Keep me safe. And in his mind, that meant for himself as well, even if it was the only thing I wanted. Damn him for that, and damn myself for loving it about him.

I sat there until my heartbeat calmed to normal speed and my legs stopped trembling before slowly returning to my room. I refused to cry over him. Not anymore, not again.

Once in my beautiful princess suite, a few tears did fall, but I told myself it was from frustration since all my hard work was going to waste because of the overprotective men in my life.

Not because Mikhail Roslov wouldn't kiss me.

Chapter 10 - Mikhail

I crashed into my bedroom and slammed the door behind me, furious that I couldn't get everything I wanted to do to Evelina out of my head. That bikini she was wearing should have been illegal, barely covering any of her silky smooth flesh.

And why did we have to start having so much fun? Frolicking in the pool with her had made me forget the last few terrible weeks and the turf war my organization had barely won.

I should have left her there on her own. The place was a fortress, so deep in the Everglades, even the most dedicated poachers never came close to it. It was surrounded by water, with three different bridges to cross, all under twenty-four-hour surveillance, before the twelve-foot high wall that ran around the entire house. I had armed guards here at all times. They could have kept her safe on the infinitesimal chance that anyone managed to breach the perimeter.

But I couldn't do it. Not if there was a chance smaller than a microbe that she might come to harm. Seeing her slip under water for a split second made my heart climb out of my chest. She was never in any danger of drowning, but I'd acted before I could think, hauling her above the surface. If the Novikoffs found her, I'd never forgive myself, and not just because of Kristina's heartbreak over losing her best friend or Oleg being devastated for losing his daughter.

I would have been devastated. She was like a—

No, not a daughter, God no. Not after how I felt when she wrapped her legs around me. Not with the way I couldn't keep my eyes off her ripe body in that swimsuit.

I paced my room, far too worked up to sleep. If I lay down and closed my eyes, visions of Evelina would only dance provocatively through my head. They were doing it right now, making me hard all over again. I was beginning to rue the moment I saw that sexy redhead in the coffee shop, planning what we'd be getting up to after I introduced myself and worked my charm on her. If only she hadn't turned around and revealed herself to be someone I could never have. And if only she wasn't so brave and stubborn and foolish to have gotten herself marked for death by a rival family.

So what was Evelina to me?

She was a favor to a friend, nothing more. And if I couldn't leave her here on her own due to my loyalty to Oleg, I needed a distraction from her. Better yet, I needed to give her a distraction to keep her from driving me up a wall.

Really, what was that at the pool? I'd been so close to losing control. No one made me feel so out of my depth until now. Was she teasing me as a punishment for interfering with her freedom? She certainly didn't have real feelings for me, did she? Or want me in the way I wanted her? It was absurd. I was literally old enough to be her—

God, I needed to stop thinking like that.

Kristina's mother and I had married when we were both very young. Kids, really. I'd only just turned twenty when Kristina was born, so I was quite a bit younger than Oleg. But I could still be Evelina's father!

But I wasn't, and she was making it very clear she didn't view me that way. I was as heated as when I'd been trapped between her creamy thighs, the vee of her bikini all but begging to be pushed aside so I could plunge my tongue inside her. If this was all a game to her, I needed to tap out, be the grown-up. Stop playing altogether. Because it had to be nothing more to her. The idea that she might be seriously interested in me was too unbelievable.

Pissed off that she was toying with me and the fact I was back to thinking about what I wanted to do with her all over again, I stormed into the bathroom and stepped under an icy shower. I turned the pressure up to pound down on my back, taking the frigid needles of pain as penance for losing control at all and hoping it would take my mind off of Evelina.

It didn't.

I really needed to come up with something to keep her occupied and get her mind off of torturing me before I made a mistake I'd regret.

CHAPTER 11 - EVELINA

After two uneventful days, I was going stir-crazy in my mansion prison, wondering when my father would pick me up. And not sure if I wanted him to or not. It wasn't like I was getting to spend any time with Mikhail. I hadn't seen or heard him since he left me at the pool. He hadn't shown up for any meals, leaving me to eat alone in the dining room like some sad billionaire orphan whose father was off working in the diamond mines.

Why did I always think of myself as a child when I thought about Mikhail? I knew I wasn't; he knew I wasn't. He was just too loyal to my father's friendship to take what I could tell he wanted. I could see it in his eyes when he was so close to kissing me at the pool. It was all I could think about. Partly because I had nothing else to do. Sure, I could read one of his many books or watch movies, but I found I couldn't sit still. I needed to work.

I'd been working since I was a teenager, doing whatever my dad would let me do for the family. I worked through college, building up my investigative business to what it was today. Leo and I were constantly coming up with ideas to make it better. I didn't like lazing around with a book or sunning by the pool. I needed to keep busy with something meaningful, but there was nothing to do.

I began to think he might have left, which didn't sit well with me, even though it might mean an opportunity to slip away. I finally gave up skulking around the pool or the area of the house where I suspected his office was and set out to do some exploring around the grounds.

Once I got past the carefully maintained area around the house, the land on the outskirts was enveloped in thorny vines and palmetto bushes that were almost as tall as I was and grew so close together I couldn't see the ground. I could almost hear all the snakes slithering around beneath their fronds. In any direction I went, it either ended in an impassable jungle or water.

It was all beautiful, and I stood staring out at the endless green water dotted with cypress trees and grasses that waved in the steamy breeze. It was definitely not like anything I'd ever seen in Russia. A bit creepy, as well as hypnotizing, watching the currents and odd bubbles while birds called to each other all around me. When a heron swooped out of the dense forest and landed on a cypress knee, I held my breath as it poked its long beak into the water. I fully expected a gator's head to rear out from the murky water and snap it in half.

I knew that the Everglades could make me disappear even more efficiently than the Novikoffs if I risked entering the wilds. I knew Mikhail enough that his stupid wall would be waiting for me if I managed to live long enough to reach it.

Thankfully the bird didn't get eaten in front of me and flapped away back into the trees. Disillusioned by the realization I wasn't getting off the island so easily, I returned to the house to see a package had arrived for me. I took it upstairs and tore into it, but as I saw the contents, my excitement at a possible gift from Mikhail faded. It was several pairs of baggy jeans, oversized sweatpants, and extra-large t-shirts. They were all good brands, and the sweats were softer than a kitten, but my feelings still took a hit.

Did he really not want me wearing his girlfriend's clothes that badly? And whether or not these new things were expensive, they were still awful. Ugly and way too large. Is that how he saw me? A big, sloppy blob?

While I certainly didn't dress as provocatively as his mysterious girlfriend with all her bodycon dresses, tiny shorts, and halters, I still liked showing off my figure. No matter how comfortable they might be, I wouldn't have been caught dead in the new clothes.

After my shower, I shoved the pile of new outfits back into their box and picked out the skimpiest dress in the closet to wear down to dinner. The gauzy white fabric fell to my knees but was almost sheer and completely backless. Not that Mikhail would show up to see my act of defiance, but it made me feel better about myself when I saw how hot I looked in the three-way mirror in the closet. My self-esteem was hard-fought over the years, and I refused to have it be shaken.

Even though I hadn't seen him in two days and was sure he wouldn't show up for dinner, I was still disappointed when he didn't. Enough to make me barely pick at the meal and sink into a fresh round of self-doubt. I was tired of feeling like there was a vice wrapped around my heart when it came to Mikhail. I'd spent most of my younger years heartsick over him. Who cared if he had a girlfriend he liked seeing in those sexy outfits, and he only thought I was suited for sweats? Who cared if he ignored me?

I did, and I was just plain over it. It was so much easier to be mad at him than feel hurt over his actions or lack of them. Just as I pushed my plate aside, my appetite completely ruined, he appeared in the doorway. I stood there, stunned as usual by his gorgeous face like I always was, no matter my mood.

He swept my scantily clad body with eyes that grew stormier with every inch he inspected. He swore under his breath, and I straightened up, thrusting out my chin. Let him look and think whatever he wanted. If he was going to keep me prisoner, I'd wear what I damn well pleased.

However, as he continued to scowl, I felt slightly anxious. Had I gone too far? I wished I could shake that absurd jealousy and that he didn't seem so wrapped up in what I wore.

"Come with me," he grunted, already turning and heading out of the dining room. Like he couldn't bear to look at me another minute.

Since these were the first words he'd said to me in two days, I followed, curiosity overtaking everything else. He stopped in the entry hall and waved to a big pile of boxes near the front door. They had to have just arrived because they weren't there when I returned from exploring.

"Open them; they're for you," he said, handing me a box cutter from one of the side tables in the foyer. His face stiff and unreadable.

I looked at the three big boxes, wondering if it was more ugly clothes. And if so, how long did he plan to keep me here? Only one way to find out. I took the knife and sliced through the top of the first box, which he helped me get down from the top of the pile. At first, all I saw was tightly packed styrofoam and wedged it out. His gruff face had tempered my curiosity, and I was unsure what to expect.

Then I saw what was under all the padding and began to hold my breath. I began to hope a little as I tore through the next box to be sure I was seeing what I was seeing. My face felt like it would crack from smiling, and actual tears welled up in my eyes.

My computer, monitors, and surveillance equipment. Cameras, microphones, and cords. It was like being reunited with my long-lost babies. I pulled my favorite keyboard out of the final box and hugged it to my chest. Mikhail laughed, and I turned to him to see him smiling as widely as I was. His stern act had been a ruse to surprise me.

And what a surprise. I blinked away the tears with a laugh, unsure what all of my things being returned to me meant.

"I don't understand," I started.

"Well, that's everything that was left in Kristina's apartment. Maybe there's a manual underneath all those cords."

I snorted at his dad joke. "No, I mean, why are you giving it back to me?"

He shrugged. "You seemed like you needed a distraction," he replied cagily.

I put the keyboard down and flung myself at him, wrapping him in a hug. "Thank you, you're the best," I said into his neck.

The moment I was flush against his hard body, all the possibilities that the arrival of my computer setup opened up melted away. He still presented a world of possibilities I was dying to explore. I held on tighter, burying my face into his shoulder and breathing him in. Usually, when I smelled his spicy cologne, I was assailed by past memories, but now I was only thinking about the future. A future I wanted him to be a part of.

"You don't know how much this means to me," I said, pressing myself closer to him. I couldn't let go.

A moment later, his hands rose to pat my back. Not what I wanted, but his touch still felt so good and right. Then he flattened his palms against my bare skin and slid them lower, pausing as they reached the point where the thin fabric covered my behind. I took a deep breath, letting my breasts rub sinuously against his chest, and sighed as I clung to him. His fingers began to curl around my ass, and I felt the first stirrings of steel against my stomach, awakening a hot pooling of lust in my core.

I turned to run my lips across his neck, but he firmly gripped my sides and took a step back. He kept his hands on my waist for a second, maybe to steady himself or both of us. My knees were certainly weak from being enclosed in his arms like that.

He pointed to the boxes, scraping his fingers through his wavy hair until it was adorably rumpled. "I hope you don't make me regret this."

He meant the computer. Right. I was already full of regret, but the sight of my beloved gear got my blood pumping in a different but still satisfying way. If I couldn't have Mikhail, at least I could salvage my project.

"Oh, you won't regret it," I said, happily pulling out cords and draping them over my shoulder. I was ready to set up right there in the entry hall.

"Hold up," he said. "I've got a room cleared for you. Let's get everything in there before you start unpacking."

Was he going to help me? Actually, spend time with me? "Just wait until you see what I've already got," I told him.

He looked at me for a long time in silence. Finally, a soft smile curled his lips. "Let's get started, then."

He picked up one of the heavy boxes, and I followed him with an armload of whatever I could grab. My heart no longer had the band around it. It felt like it was soaring, and not just because I had all my equipment back.

CHAPTER 12 - MIKHAIL

Seeing the overjoyed look on Evelina's face was the most satisfying thing I'd seen in a long while, and that should have already unsettled me. I'd sent for her computer, thinking this would just keep her out of trouble and out of my sight and mind.

Watching her tear through the packaging like it was Christmas morning gave me a deep feeling of contentment. It was so easy to make her happy; I was already devising more ways to hear that coo of excitement and put that light in her eyes. When she threw herself into my arms, I couldn't resist holding onto her for just a second.

Her sweet, soft body just seemed to fit perfectly with mine, and she smelled like the expensive shampoo and lotions I'd had her room stocked with. Oh, she was tempting, and my hands acted without permission from my brain. That organ checked out the second she breathed her thanks into my neck. Her warm breath tickled my earlobe and had my heart kicking up a notch.

Finding satisfaction in her smiles was one thing, but this was taking it a bit too far. My body began to respond to her, my fingers curling into the plush mounds of her ass cheeks, barely covered by one of the most outrageous dresses yet. My cock was waking up, and my control was slipping again. Hadn't the less tempting clothes I ordered arrived yet? Or was she still trying to seduce me?

Trying and succeeding.

I pushed away. The lack of her heat against me shook me, and I had to steady myself. Good thing she now had something to keep her busy.

Setting up that jumble of electronics would take her a good few days, and I'd be able to stop hiding out in my suite.

Yes, she could do her own thing and give up her little game of making my life a living hell with her gorgeous curves on full display. Now was the time I should have left her to it, maybe called one of the guards to help her carry everything to her new office, but my feet wouldn't move from their spot in the hall. My eyes wouldn't move from her big, joyous smile.

"Just wait until you see what I've already got," she bragged, wrapping herself in cords and trying to carry far too much at once.

She was not just irresistible because of her nearly sheer dress. Her restless yearning to succeed was infectious, and suddenly taking down the Novikoffs was the only thing I wanted, too. Or at least humoring her. Of course, she couldn't do anything new, but hopefully, combing through the data she had already gathered would be enough for now.

Before I knew it, I was offering to help, one of the big boxes already hoisted in my arms. With a squeal of delight that threatened to wake my cock up again, I moved faster, meaning to get the boxes in and get out.

Until she kicked off her high heels and started unpacking, handing me things, and giving orders like the world's sexiest drill sergeant. I couldn't have left that room if a gun was to my head, but I tried to tell myself she needed help. She might get hurt. Anything but the truth, which was that I wanted to spend time with her.

I was mostly relegated to holding cords and lifting the heavier monitors. And watching her flit around from piece to piece, leaning over to attach cords, fiddling with where everything went. She chattered away about what each thing was, but I could barely understand why I was so enamored by her. When was the last time I was so focused and passionate about something in the way Evelina was about her work?

If ever, it had been a long time. The years of being a killing machine, always seeking and gaining power, then brawling like a frenzied shark to keep it, had made me a bit jaded. A bit hardened. Evelina's softness, mixed with her eager ambition, was like a balm to a wound I didn't realize I had.

And dear God, was she sexy in that dress, though she acted like she was wearing jeans and a t-shirt, completely oblivious to her effect on me.

I needed to stop staring at her, or she might notice and get the wrong idea. Or the right idea.

To get past my confusion, I grabbed the cords she needed to be plugged in and crawled under the desk. I needed a break to calm myself down and to keep her from bending over and waving her pert ass in the air like a flag she wanted me to capture.

She handed me a tangled handful of wires and started reeling off instructions. Looking at the wires and cords and then the back of the tower computer, I knew I was in over my head.

"So, will something explode if I do it wrong?"

"You can't do it wrong," she laughed, leaning down to peer at me with a teasing smile. I blinked in wonder at her breasts about to spill out of her dress and hurriedly turned my attention back to the cords. "They'll only fit where they're supposed to fit."

I poked the ends of the computer. "No, this one has three choices. And this one won't fit anywhere on here."

She sighed. "That one goes in the power strip, Grandpa. Haven't you ever set up a computer before?"

I narrowed my eyes at her for the grandpa crack. "Watch it," I growled. "And no, I pay people to do work like this."

"Then you're missing out on the joys of getting your hands dirty," she said, kneeling down and pushing her way under the desk with me.

She deftly separated the plugs and had them attached in no time, but her expertise wasn't what held me in thrall. Having her on her hands and knees, her dress hitched up her thighs, and her soft skin brushing against me in the confined space was working every last shred of my sanity. When she was done, she turned to me in triumph. I barely got my eyes up in time and smirked at her giggle as she realized our awkward position.

I couldn't edge out without her moving first, and she stayed as still as a statue, our bodies pressed together while she searched my face. Our eyes locked and stayed that way, and I barely noticed anymore where we were at, only that we were touching.

"Thank you for this," she said quietly.

A moment later, my mouth was on hers, parting her lips with my tongue as I reached for her. My hand slid up the side of her neck and into her hair. Her fingers curled into my shirt, her knuckles pressing against my rapidly beating heart. I couldn't have said who leaned in first, only that I liked the taste of her. Far too much. Her soft moan mingled with one of my own as I pulled her closer, roughly, hungrily. At war.

This wasn't someone I met in a bar. She wasn't that mysterious redhead from the coffee shop who'd be perfect for a fling and wouldn't care if we never saw each other again. Evelina was someone I already knew. Someone who was important to me. That scared the hell out of me. It also caused a sharp stab of sadness.

I couldn't remember the last time I had a serious relationship, one based on mutual interests, love, and trust. Ever since Kristina's mother ran out on us, I had closed myself off to keep from being so thoroughly fooled by a woman again, unable to trust enough to have deep feelings for anyone.

Did I think I had those kinds of feelings for Evelina? Something thrummed between us that was almost palpable as our hands searched for each other and our tongues tangled. Something that wasn't just pent-up lust. I couldn't deal with it, but I couldn't pull away, either. We were magnetized.

"Mikhail," she murmured as I dragged my lips across her cheek to lick the side of her throat. "Oh my God, Mikhail…"

Hearing her say my name in that breathy tone, not angry or sarcastic or teasing, made me throb almost painfully. Her hand smoothed its way down my chest to rest at the top of my jeans, and her sharp intake of breath to feel how much I wanted her made me smile against her neck.

I tugged her hair back, my other hand finding her breast and closing around the firm mound. Her nipple tightened beneath my palm, making me jerk her closer to me. With a crash, we tumbled out from under the desk. The evening light from the high windows made her blink as she landed beneath me. Shock at having her in a position I'd been thinking about far too much the last few days made me pause and look down at her.

Her lips were slightly swollen from our rough, fevered kisses, her hair tousled, and her green eyes glazed with the same desire I was once again trying to fight. Too much blood was being diverted from my brain to think clearly. Not when she was reaching for me and once again whispering my name.

She spread her legs, revealing a scrap of sheer white panties, damp and clinging to her pussy. I groaned as she quickly wrapped her legs around me, pulling me down to her chest. She gripped my shoulders and tipped her chin back, licking her lips. All but begging me to enter her mouth again.

"Please don't stop this time." She was actually begging me.

My mind went blank. A white room with nothing but her gorgeous body spread out beneath me, her hands pulling me close. Her mouth was open and needy for my tongue. My own need for her was strong, too strong to fight anymore.

"Nothing could stop me," I assured her, dipping my head to taste her again. "You're so sweet, Evelina. Like honey on my tongue."

Her arms tightened around my back as she writhed beneath me. My cock throbbed stiffly between her thighs, so ready. As I kissed her, she arched her back, seeming to beg some more with her body. But I had been thinking about this to the point of distraction. Just because I was crazed with wanting her, finally so close to having her, didn't mean I wasn't going to make her enjoy every second of it. And make it last for a good long time.

Maybe I wanted a little revenge. Maybe I just wanted to mark her indelibly.

I tore myself from her lips and worked my way down her throat, smiling as she sighed and tipped her head back to give me better access. At her chest, I tugged at the thin fabric of the dress tormenting me, finally tearing it down the middle. Her luscious breasts were mine to lick and caress, and I dipped my head to draw a taut nipple into my mouth.

She shivered beneath me, running her fingers through my hair and finally gripping tight as I continued to tease her.

"Tell me what you want next," I said, glancing up at her to find her biting her lip.

Her chest heaved, and she pushed my head further down. "I want more of that, but everywhere, Mikhail."

"Good," I told her.

Just what I wanted as well. She wriggled her shoulders to work the straps down, but I was too impatient. The dress was already ruined, so I continued ripping it open to reveal the curve of her stomach. I dipped my tongue into her belly button, eliciting a sharp giggle that she quickly stifled.

"Don't be quiet. I want to hear everything I make you feel," I commanded.

She nodded and let her head drop back onto the rug, the sunshine streaming through the windows still dappling her pretty features. My beautiful, golden girl.

"She's not going to like what you did to the dress," she murmured as I traced the curve of her hip on my way lower.

"What? Who?" I asked, frowning.

She shook her head. "Nothing, don't stop."

"This dress is yours, baby. Everything upstairs is for you."

Her hands landed on my shoulders as she half sat up. "What? They're not for another woman?"

"Why would they be?" I reached to press her back down, eager to get back to kissing my way down her body. "Be quiet and let me lick you, little girl." I leaned up on my elbow and ran my fingertip between her thighs, up and down her slit, through the soaked panties. "When I get down here, I'm going to rip these off, too."

She drew in a ragged breath, still half sitting but staring at where my finger continued to work up and down between her legs.

"Then what?" she asked breathlessly.

I chuckled. "Wait and see."

She gripped my shoulder. "No, tell me." When I dragged my gaze from the crux of her thighs to her face, her cheeks were blushing a delightful bright pink, but her green eyes were intense. "N-no one's ever talked dirty to me before," she said, barely above a whisper.

Well, that was a shame, and I felt a surge of proprietorship over her. A desire to show her what a grown man could make her feel. In short, to give her whatever she wanted. I increased the pressure of my teasing strokes, pulling the tiny scrap of panties tight against her until she gasped. This was going to be fun.

"I'm going to put my fingers inside your tight little hole," I said. "And you're going to beg me for my cock." Her face grew redder, and she looked down, but I sat up and took my free hand to grip her chin, not allowing her to be shy now. I found her swollen nub beneath the stretched-tight fabric and began to slowly circle. "I'm going to suck your clit until you scream, and while you're coming, I'm going to lap up your wet pussy like an ice cream cone."

She swallowed hard and nodded with my fingers still gripping her chin, her chest rising and falling faster as I kept circling with my fingers. As much as I wanted to keep toying with her, I needed more. Much more.

"How wet is your pussy already?" I asked. "Tell me."

"Find out for yourself," she whimpered, dragging her face from my grasp and flopping back onto the rug. "Oh, please, Mikhail. Do those things right now."

With barely a flick of my wrist, the panties were off, her body was completely open to me. Her pussy glistened as she lifted her hips, eager for everything I promised. God, I was harder than steel, about to come in my pants at the vision before me. It was as if she transported me back to my youth, as eager as she was and ready to blow.

I slid two fingers inside her, groaning at the hot, wet feel of her tight channel, groaning again as she writhed against my questing touch. "Beg me," I said. "Like I told you."

"I—I need your cock inside me," she said, boldly looking up. "I need you to fuck me now."

I smiled and shook my head. "Not yet. You know what's next."

She squeezed her eyes shut and nodded, reaching for my hair as I lowered my head between her thighs. I spread her legs further and claimed her swollen clit between my lips, reaching up for her breast—wanting and needing every inch of her. Her hand clapped over mine to guide it, and I rolled her hard little nipple between my thumb and finger.

"Yessss," she purred, moving my hand with hers, back and forth over her perfect tits.

Her hips bucked, and I looked up to admonish her to be still, but her eyes were still closed, and her head was thrown back. She was so close to ecstasy and so very gorgeous in her pleasure. I held her hips tightly so she couldn't move and forced her over the edge. I'd told her what I was going to do to her body and how she would respond. If she wanted to continue, I needed to hear her—

The scream echoed throughout the big, airy room, and she struggled to move under my firm hold, but I wasn't done with her yet. Her whole body shook with the force of her orgasm as her shouts faded into moans, and her arms fell limp at her sides.

"I still get to lick up your juices, baby," I said, lapping down her slit and shoving my tongue deep inside her.

Soon her hands found my hair again, and she pulled instead of pushed this time. "More," she gasped. "You know what I need."

"Do I?" I asked.

Her lower lip jutted out in a pout, and she sat up, leaning on her trembling arms. After a deep breath, she shoved me back to a sitting position and wrapped her hand around my cock.

"Fuck," I said, gritting my teeth. Holy, holy fuck.

"That's what I want," she said, her voice more sure now. "Looks like the same thing you do."

I loved having her at my mercy, but I loved this less submissive side of her too. And I really loved the way she slid her hand up and down my shaft, running her thumb back and forth over the dripping tip. The smile on her face was downright mischievous. God, who was this girl? No, who was this woman?

She shifted to her knees and leaned over to tentatively lick me, her sexy ass in the air. I let her run her tongue up and down my length but stopped her when her lips wrapped around the tip, and she began to suck.

"Let me," she whined. I never thought I'd ever hear a sexy whine, but Evelina managed it. "Let me suck your big cock, Mikhail."

I groaned and wrapped my arms around her waist, and flipped her onto her back again. "Oh, little girl, I'd love to, but right about now, I'd shoot straight down your throat with how much I want you." I eased my fingers back inside her, watching her eyes roll back in her head. "And I thought you wanted me to fuck this sweet pussy of yours."

Her eyes flew open, and she smiled, reaching down to help guide me to her opening. "Yes, so much. So much."

Some form of logic was trying to break through the haze of lust that enveloped us, but I could only feel the tip of my cock about to enter Evelina's body. Her gorgeous, voluptuous body that she was offering to me. I could only concentrate on making her mine. With a single long, hard thrust, I was enveloped deep inside her pussy. Her legs locked around my waist, and she grabbed my jaw to pull me down for a kiss. I gave her every inch as I slid my tongue between her ready lips.

Now that I had claimed her, it was impossible to hold back. The urge to completely make her mine was primal, deep. As deep as I was ramming my cock inside her. She held onto my shoulders, burying her face against my neck as I pounded her body. When she began to pant and dig her fingernails into my back, I lost the last shred of control. Propping myself up on my elbow, I slid my free hand between our sweat-slicked bodies and nudged my fingers down her smooth mound to find that sweet, swollen nub I loved playing with.

No sooner had my fingers slid across her clit than she screamed again, and when she spasmed around my cock, I let loose, spilling my seed inside her. Every last drop until I was spent and fell against her chest. Breathless and utterly sated.

"Christ, your body is amazing," I said, rolling off and cradling her to me.

"I can't wait to do it again," she said between panting breaths.

I pressed my hand to her heart to feel the racing beats, and she leaned close and kissed my jaw. This was …

Something. Reality slowly crept in as my heart rate settled and my breathing slowed. I wasn't lying naked with a woman I met at the local bar. This woman who had her leg slung across mine, whose body I had just tasted, touched, and fucked until she screamed and raked her fingers down my back, was Evelina Morozov.

Oh fuck, I'd done the unthinkable with my best friend's daughter. I was as good as a dead man. And God help me, I'd been so crazed with desire for her hot little body that I hadn't thought twice about taking her without a condom! I deserved to be shot.

"What's wrong?" she asked.

I had gone still, my arms and legs like lead. I was furious enough to pick up the big desk we'd started all this foolishness under and throw it through the windows. But not at her, never at her. At myself for losing control. For my utter weakness where she was concerned. I could have told her not to wear the skin-tight, flimsy outfits, but damn it, I liked looking at her body.

I should have continued staying away from her, but I liked her company too, and those two days without speaking to her when I knew she was all alone in this giant house slashed at me like razors.

I slowly extricated myself from her embrace, one I could have happily died in if she were anyone else. But she wasn't anyone else.

"Are you sure everything's okay?" she asked as I tugged my jeans back up and pulled my shirt into place.

I would have rather taken a knife to the gut than hurt her feelings after she'd so thoroughly given herself to me, but this couldn't continue. It shouldn't have started, but that was on me. That was my burden to bear.

"I should probably let you get back to setting up," I said, easing toward the door. The look of confusion and hurt in her eyes made me turn away.

"You're not going to help anymore?" she asked, trying to pull what was left of her dress around her.

God, I needed to be shot. "I, uh, have some things I need to do."

Before I could hear her voice again, I hurried out the door, despising myself for my depravity and, worse, cowardice.

Chapter 13 - Evelina

The switch happened fast, and it pissed me off. One minute we were snuggling and sweaty on the floor. My body still tingled from everything he did, everything he said, and my heartbeat was only just evening out. It was official. No other man on earth could do what he did to me. I was still half floating up in the clouds, dreamily lost in the aftershocks of those absolutely earth-shattering orgasms he gave me when he started getting stiff.

And not in the good way that might signify another round. No, he was thinking. Starting to war with himself. Probably have regrets. He was ruining everything about the very best sexual encounter I ever had. The thought that it might be the last if he came to the stupid conclusion he'd made a mistake was enough to get my heart racing again. And this time, not with ecstasy.

And now he was slithering out the door without a backward glance? Hell no.

My damn dress was in tatters, but the small couch in the corner had a cashmere blanket thrown over the back. I grabbed it, wrapped it around myself, and chased him to the hall. He turned and gaped at seeing me naked and wrapped in a throw and quickly looked around for any of the meandering security guards who mostly kept to the shadows but were always there.

I didn't give a single solitary damn if anyone saw me and put two and two together. I wasn't going to be his dirty little secret! Not when we were so perfect together. He could lie to himself, but I could read his eyes as easily as a toddler's picture book. His eyes showed everything. Then and now. Then they'd been full of passion, desire, and maybe even joy. Now they gleamed with regret, just as I suspected.

If only he'd figured it out, he would regret running much more than losing his precious control around me.

He took me by the shoulders with a scowl and pushed me back into the office. "Good," I said. "Glad you decided to see reason."

His scowl grew darker, but I wasn't afraid of him. Not when so much was on the line. What we'd done was better than I ever could have imagined. And I spent a lot of years imagining being with him.

"Don't," he said when I refused to cower under his fierce glare.

"No, you don't," I answered right back. "Don't run away like that."

"Evelina, I'm not—"

"Yes, you are. You forget I know you as well as you know me."

His shoulders slumped, and his hands fell to his sides. He'd been holding onto me in anger, but I still missed his touch once it was gone.

"That's the problem," he said. "The fact that we know each other. I watched you grow up, for God's sake."

"You need to fuck off with that nonsense," I said, laughing at his shocked reaction. "What? I can say the word when I'm begging you to do it to me, but not when you're acting like an ass?"

"Evelina," he groaned. I was getting to him. Good.

"I'm a grown woman," I reminded him, making him roll his eyes. "Not the little girl you used to pick up from school. Do you think I'm incapable of making my own decisions? Or too stupid to know what I want?"

He closed his eyes and muttered under his breath as if he was praying for guidance. "I don't think you're incapable or stupid," he sighed. "Far from either."

"Then what is it?"

He was still maddeningly closed off, and yet, all I wanted was for him to gather me back into his arms.

"It's nothing," he said, backing out the door again. "I'm tired. I put things off to help you with your setup. Things I need to get finished."

Well, that was a whole lot of excuses. It was clear he was done talking to me.

"Mikhail," I pleaded. One last ditch effort to salvage our beautiful moment together.

"Good night," he said, turning away.

I stepped out into the hall and silently watched him go up the stairs and then round the corner. He never once looked back. Ruined. Over. I'd finally gotten what I wanted from him, and it had been better than all my dreams, but I almost wished it never happened.

Because it hurt like a son of a bitch. I was born into a mafia family. I could take a punch. I'd even had a minor stab wound once by some lowlife I tracked down and brought in for the bounty. This was every blow, every insult, every heartbreak rolled into a ball. Then it inflated until it popped, littering pain all over me. I couldn't move. I couldn't breathe.

I refused to cry.

I turned back and shut myself into the room that was supposed to be my office. I might as well get back to work. Work never betrayed me or let me down. If something went wrong with a camera or a glitch in a program, I figured it out and fixed it. Why couldn't things with Mikhail be as simple as setting up my monitors?

Once everything was hooked up properly and firing up, I was a little less shell-shocked. But I knew I didn't want to stay here any longer. My father still hadn't come to get me for some unknown reason, which had been fine because I didn't want to go back to Moscow until now. Now I'd go anywhere as long as it wasn't here. All I had to do was get a message out to Leo, and he'd find a way to pick me up. Yes, I still had my brother, and while he wanted to keep me safe, if I told him I was truly miserable here, he'd get me out.

There had to be other places I could hide out until the heat with the Novikoffs was off. One of my cousins' places or their many secret safe houses. Or they could let me figure it out and solve my own problems for once. I was still wallowing in pain, which made me laugh since it would never happen.

Not until I proved somehow that I was more than just their surveillance expert. And having my computer back was the first step in the right direction. I loaded up all my programs, fiddling with settings, and became increasingly irritated. Why couldn't I connect to the internet?

After twenty fruitless minutes of running diagnostics, I had to accept I wasn't able to connect. Something was wrong, and I blamed Mikhail. It would be just like him to dangle a carrot like my equipment, all the while knowing he wasn't going to let me take a bite.

I stormed upstairs, realizing I still had the blanket on, tied like a toga over my shoulder. That happened when I got in the zone and completely lost track of reality. Swearing, I switched directions to my room and pulled on a pair of the hated sweatpants and my own t-shirt, which had been magically laundered and returned to me.

Crashing back to his room, I pounded on the door until he swung it open. He had his phone in his hand and was clearly distracted, barely glancing at me except to raise a questioning eyebrow before turning his attention right back to his phone. He was freshly out of a shower, with slicked-back wet hair that still dripped a bit on his bare shoulders and track pants slung low on his lean hips. I tore my interest from his rippling abs, remembering what I was there for.

"I can't do anything without the internet," I said. He nodded absently, his brows drawn together as he scrolled through a long message. "Hello, Mikhail? All that equipment downstairs might as well be paperweights without internet access."

He finally looked up at me, holding out his phone. "Ivan's house was raided an hour ago."

Stricken by that news, my thoughts swiveled to my cousin, his wife, and their precious little daughter. "Are they okay? What happened?" My heart sank. Was it the Novikoffs? Was the attack because of me?

"Read for yourself."

I grabbed his phone and scrolled through the message, skipping over words in my haste to assure myself I hadn't caused any harm to my family. They'd been nothing but welcoming and kind to me, and I'd brought havoc to them because of my ambitions and greed. I felt my knees giving out, and Mikhail grabbed my elbow to keep me upright. After a calming breath, I reread the message.

Someone had breached the perimeter of their mansion on the waterway, probably coming in by boat. They'd set off an explosive device at the outer wall and then started a fire as a distraction so someone could get into the house. Thankfully they hadn't succeeded, but the intruders managed to get away, so no punishments could be meted out, and no one knew for sure who it was who'd tried such a thing. Everyone was okay, and they were heading to their holiday home in the Keys until things settled down.

"Was this because of me?" I asked, hoping to hear anything but the truth. Mikhail remained silent because we both knew it was. "Does that mean they know I'm in Miami?"

"They can't know for certain; I made sure of that. But they must suspect because of your family ties here."

I started to shake, realizing how easily it could have been different news that Mikhail got. That Ivan and his family might be dead because of me.

He pulled me close and rubbed my back to try to calm my tremors. "Don't worry. You're perfectly safe."

"But my family isn't," I said against his chest. The tears I'd fought so valiantly began to well up again, but I blinked them away. Then pushed out of his embrace, as comforting as it was. That wasn't what I needed right now. "They're not going to be safe until I put a stop to the Novikoffs for good." I looked up at him with all the ferocity I could muster. "And for that, I need internet access.

"Ah, Evelina," he said, running a finger down my face. "You're clearly worn out."

"I'm fine," I argued, but suddenly felt like I'd been hit by a bus. I had to swallow a huge yawn.

"It's the middle of the night," he told me, waving to the clock on his bedside table. Squinting, I saw he was right. It was almost two in the morning. I'd been working so hard that I lost track of time again. "A good night's sleep will make you sharper."

He was right about that too, and I expected him to push me out the door, but to my surprise, he led me over to his bed and pulled the covers back. The fluffy pillows looked enticing, but was he going to get in alongside me? I gave him a quizzical look, but the lure of the pure white sheets was too strong to ask silly questions. I got in and sighed, stretching my feet as far as they would go and wiggling my toes against the cool cotton.

He snickered and pulled the comforter over me, then shook his head and lay down on top of the blankets next to me.

"Oh, that's very respectable," I said, rolling onto my side to look at him, staring at the ceiling.

"Hush and go to sleep," he grumbled.

But I wasn't tired anymore, not with him lying shirtless next to me. He would have been far less enticing if he'd gotten under the covers where I couldn't see his pecs, but then again, all I would have to do was reach over and touch him. I started to worm my way out, but he reached his arm over and slapped it down on the weighty comforter, preventing me from moving.

My top half, anyway. I slid my leg out and swung it across his knees, rolling with all my might until my head rested on his chest.

"Might as well let me be comfortable," I said.

He laughed and gave in, whipping back the blanket and ducking under it. With a resigned sigh, he moved his arm around me, letting me get nice and close.

"Comfortable enough?" he asked.

I had a question of my own, namely, why was he being so nice to me? Like he said, I was in no danger on his compound. I wouldn't have asked it for the world; just happy to be back in his arms. Of course, I knew I was courting more pain, but I'd always been one to live in the moment. I wriggled closer until my front was flush with his side and slipped my hand onto his flat stomach. I only meant to rest it there, but the hot, firm flesh made my fingers move on their own. I stroked up and down his hard abs, going a little higher to feel his chest hair under my palm, then sliding lower until I felt the waistband of his pants.

"What are you doing?" he asked softly.

Not angry, not gruff. I would have guessed I was lulling him to sleep if I hadn't felt the tip of his erection against the edge of my thumb.

"Counting your abs," I said, tipping my chin up to see if he was drifting off to sleep. "To see if you really have a six-pack."

He snorted. Wide awake. Just like I was. My body was relaxed against his, but inside I was coiled and ready to strike. My skin almost crackled, like I was caught out in an electrical storm, waiting for him to touch me.

"You can see I have more like an eight-pack," he said indignantly.

"Yeah, you look great." I kept watching his face, warmed by his smile.

He finally looked down at me, and the smile faded as his eyes darkened. I let my hand wander lower, waiting for him to stop me when I kept moving down past his waistband over the thick bulge that strained the fabric. I swallowed hard, feeling like I was parched. Not for a drink, but what only he could give me. How many hours had it been since he took me to those heights? Far too long.

He didn't stop me but tangled his fingers in my hair to tug my head further back. God, I loved when he did that. Loved how he took control. I ached for him and ground my body against his side as I gripped his throbbing cock. My lips parted as he leaned down to kiss me, his tongue tracing between them and making me moan.

"Touch me," I pleaded between his kisses. I needed to feel his hands on my body before I burned up.

"Take your clothes off," he replied.

I scrambled out from under the covers and stripped my sweatpants off, for once glad they were so huge that they slid off easily. He sat up and slid his own track pants down, and I moaned again at the sight of his cock nearly standing straight up. I slung my leg over to straddle him, pushing on his chest until he was lying down again. I smiled down at him as I rubbed my sensitive pussy against his iron shaft.

He grabbed my hips and held me still, his eyes going from my frustrated face to my shirt with a frown. "Take off your top so I can see your tits," he said. "Then play with them for me."

I nearly passed out from giddiness but quickly complied with the first part of his command. "You have to let me move," I said, needing that friction. "Please."

He acted like he was thinking about it while gently tweaking my nipples to tight peaks. As soon as he took his hands off my hips, I knew I could have started grinding on him again, but I waited for permission. The naughtiness of letting him dominate me made my cheeks grow hot, and I couldn't hide my nervous giggle.

"It's funny how you seem to like me to tell you what to do when you're naked," he said, still driving me crazy by running his thumbs back and forth across my breasts. "Maybe I should keep you naked all the time."

"Only if we're always doing this," I countered.

He raised his eyebrows and smirked. My hips twitched to try to quell the ache between my thighs as his rock-hard cock pulsed against me.

"Don't move," he ordered. I stayed stock still, my muscles shaking as I fought the urge to rise up and slam his cock inside me and ride him until we both passed out. He nodded. "Good girl. Now give me a show, and you can rub your hot little pussy on my cock as much as you want."

"Thank you," I breathed, pushing down on him as I did what he wanted and began to stroke my breasts while he watched.

After a moment, I grew bolder and let my fingers trail up and down my sides, finally leaning over so he could take my nipple into his mouth. "That's so good," I mumbled, staring at the wall but seeing nothing. With a chuckle, he gently pushed me back up.

"You are so damn gorgeous," he said, his gaze moving up and down my body. "I can't decide if I like looking at you or licking you more."

"You can do both," I said, frantically moving my hips. "I think I need you inside me now."

He shook his head, sliding his hand down my front and between my legs. The barest nudge against my swollen clit made me nearly rear off of him. I jolted forward and held onto his shoulders as he moved his fingers back and forth in slow circles.

"Tell me how that makes you feel, little girl," he said, taking my chin and making me look at his eyes, not down where his fingers were working their magic on my body.

I shivered, finding it hard to talk as the delicious sensation built. "Good," I gasped. "So good."

I wanted release; at the same time, I wanted it to last forever, and gritted my teeth. "Mikhail, tell me what you want to do to me," I said. "Like—like last time." Yes, my cheeks were burning, but at the same time, I'd never felt so free. I would have never been so brazen with anyone but him.

"I'm already doing it," he said. "Feeling your wet pussy under my fingertips makes me so damn hard." He pushed his fingers inside me, moving them in and out. "I fucking love how wet I can make you."

"All you have to do is look at me," I confessed.

He swore softly, pushing deeper. "This tight little hole of yours is going to make me feel so good when I slam my cock into you."

I trembled almost violently, holding on to drag out every second of his expert touch. "Do it," I begged.

"Come for me first," he said, his own voice starting to sound as ragged as mine. "Right now."

Another swipe of his thumb across my clit, and I did just what he asked, what I'd been holding back like a miser with a pot of gold. As the orgasm rocked through my body, I opened my mouth and screamed. My head fell back, and I stared blindly once again, letting the bliss waves wash over me. I heard him open the bedside table drawer and fumble for something while his hand moved between my thighs. Still coaxing every last bit of pleasure.

I looked down to see him slide a condom on, and I grabbed his cock and helped him guide it inside me. With the last bit of my strength, I held on and rode him, taking every inch exactly how I wanted.

He reached for my breasts with a pained expression, groaning about how I was killing him, but I couldn't stop. As spent as I was, I was also exhilarated. As weak in the knees, as he made me with his touch, I'd never felt so powerful.

"All right, cowgirl," he finally said, grabbing me by the waist and hoisting me off of him. "Time for a switch up."

Before I could complain, he had me on my stomach, sliding into me from behind. He pressed kisses along the top of my back, his smooth, sure strokes building up my tension again. I cried out with every thrust, begging for more.

"You can have everything I've got," he said, making my heart swell.

I buried my face in the pillow as he pushed his hand under my belly to find my clit again. I was about to tip over the edge, and his slightest touch made me buck up against him and scream into the pillow while he railed me with his final, hard thrust.

"Oh my God," I said, turning my face to the side when he collapsed on top of me.

He kissed the side of my neck. "Agreed. Oh my fucking God. What is it with us?"

I couldn't hold back a smile that I wasn't the only one who thought what we had was out of this world. Certainly, he'd had much more experience than me, so I was pleased I didn't disappoint him. Now if only he wouldn't freak out again.

With our breathing back to normal, he rolled off me and lay on his back, his arms spread wide. I pulled myself closer and rested my cheek against his chest, my eyes growing heavy. He snapped the covers over us and let out a long, heady sigh as his arm wrapped around me.

"In the morning, we'll figure things out," he said.

At least that's what I thought he said because I was already well on my way to the best sleep of my life.

Chapter 14 - Mikhail

I slowly woke up from the most erotic dream of my life to realize it wasn't a dream. Evelina lay curled up beside me, the curve of her breast peeking out over the top of the blanket. Her dark lashes contrasted starkly against her pale skin, and I slowly eased onto my side to watch her sleep. Just for a moment because she looked so innocent and peaceful.

Her mouth wasn't set in stubborn lines; her brow wasn't furrowed with worry. She looked completely content, and I liked to think I had a little something to do with that. And she was so very beautiful with her hair strewn across the pillow.

I shouldn't have been waking up next to her or letting her into my bed in the first place. But she was shaken by the attack on her cousin's house and seemed to blame herself. I didn't want her to be alone, beating herself up over it. I had started out with the best of intentions.

But of course, that was what the road to hell was paved with, and it didn't take long until I was under her spell once more. How was she so irresistible to me? Was I just trying to prove to myself that our first explosive time together had been a fluke? She was forbidden fruit, after all. Lush, ripe, forbidden fruit I couldn't wait to taste. Surely the next time would be tame in comparison.

Instead, it was a hundred times more explosive. The way her body reacted to mine, the way she and I seemed to be on the same wavelength at all times, everything about being with her was better than I could have imagined. And God help me, ever since she came back into my life, I'd had more than a few fantasies about her.

Reality being so much better made me weak. Watching her now weakened me again, and I reached for her smooth shoulder. Stopping myself, I hurried out of bed. Waking up beside her was much too bizarre, and I needed to get my wits about me before she woke up.

Striding naked to the bathroom, I stepped under the shower, blasting the water until it turned cold. Only then did I think I had the fortitude to face her without spreading her thighs and diving between them.

Back in the bedroom, my bed was empty, the covers neatly pulled up over the pillows. I should have been relieved to not have to test my willpower, but I was disappointed to see she was gone. I forced myself not to look for her immediately but took my time shaving and getting dressed. There were people I needed to check in with, not least of all Evelina's father, but I couldn't stay away from her any longer and went to look for her.

The cook informed me she had grabbed an orange and disappeared. I did the same, not wanting to waste time over a full breakfast if Evelina wasn't going to join me. I strolled out to the pool and through the garden, pretending I wasn't still looking for her, finally sticking my head into her office.

She stood at the window, her hands on her hips as she turned to shake her head at me. "It's about time," she said. What was she so impatient about now? She waved me over and slid into her computer chair. "As soon as I'm connected, I can start downloading my backups and show you what I've collected so far."

I suppressed a groan when I realized she still wanted to bring down the Novikoffs, surprised to see she expected me to help her. She smiled at me, but it didn't reach her eyes.

"You didn't think I'd forget about it, did you? You weren't trying to distract me last night, were you?"

I almost laughed. After all my justifications to excuse sleeping with her, I'd never considered that one. "You're really determined, aren't you?"

She nodded vigorously. "You know I am. And once you see everything for yourself, you'll understand why. I'm really close, Mikhail."

My mind raced like a hamster on a wheel, not really going anywhere. She was safe with me. What could it really hurt to give her internet access? If I thought things were starting to go off the rails, I could easily cut her off. And her enthusiasm made me curious to see what she'd found out about this enemy that was growing a bit too bold. Despite having no proof yet, they had most certainly been behind the attack on Ivan's family home.

Not one of his many businesses, his home. It could have easily gone much worse than it did, and the Morozovs were my family's ally—my friends. If the Novikoffs figured out Evelina was with me, my organization would be next. It was very close to personal now.

"Fine," I said, taking out my phone to tell my head of security to turn the router back on.

She gaped at me. "You had it turned off in the whole house? You didn't have any internet either?"

I laughed at her. "And somehow I survived. You know you haven't had your phone since you've been with me, and you're still alive."

She rubbed her arms and scowled. "I'm all itchy, though." A second later, she snickered, but I thought she was at least half serious.

Once she was connected, her fingers flew like slender hummingbirds across her keyboard, her vision laser-focused on her screens as her head darted back and forth between them. While she worked, she filled me in on what was happening. Something had to download, something else had to update.

I sat across from her desk, as enthralled as if watching a thriller. After about half an hour, she leaned back and clapped her hands.

"I can't believe it," she said, beaming. "I still have control of some of their cameras. They must be absolute idiots. If I found out someone had even one of my security cameras, I would have checked each and every last one of the others." She shrugged. "Thank goodness for stupidity, I guess."

I got up and moved to stand behind her, and she pointed out the camera feeds on one screen. Nothing much was happening, but she assured me she had started recording for when something did, then showed me the data she had collected during her time in New York. She had digital copies of everything from building deeds to bank records. I had to admit I was impressed.

"What now?" I asked, moving back to my chair. Watching her work was far more intriguing than what little was going on onscreen at the moment.

"We wait," she said with a shrug. "Surveillance isn't always that interesting. It's mostly pretty boring, actually. Until something happens, that is."

With her head bent over her keyboard, she told me she needed to update a few more things. While she worked, she had me set up her printer so she could get hard copies to take notes on, admitting with a pretty blush that she knew it was old school, but she liked to write longhand sometimes.

"It's kind of romantic," she said, scrawling her name on a stack of sticky notes.

"You need to get out more," I joked.

"Then take me out," she countered immediately.

Things threatened to get tense when I didn't know how to answer. Would I have liked to take her out to a nice dinner? Of course. Could I? Maybe with her father or brother in tow, but the way she wanted? Probably not. Definitely not. I changed the subject to less volatile things, and as she worked, we kept up a light banter, and I helped out wherever I could.

Even though they were important parts of our lives, we carefully dodged any mention of either her father or my daughter. We'd landed on a delicate truce that couldn't possibly last, but I wanted to try living in the moment. And it was a very nice moment indeed.

Until my phone rang. "It's your father," I said, not wanting to answer it.

"Don't answer it," she said, alarmed.

I laughed ruefully, accepting the call. I was aware of Evelina hanging on my every word and straining to hear what Oleg had to say on his end. I assured him everything was fine, and he apologized profusely for not getting on the plane to Miami yet.

"I had a flight planned, and someone must have gotten word I'd be out of town for a few days and tried to intercept a convoy of mine."

"Vodka?" I asked.

"Of course, vodka," he replied. "If they hadn't screwed up the day I was supposed to leave, I'd be out close to a hundred grand right now."

"Crack some heads?" I asked, wishing I hadn't. My head would be next if he ever found out what I'd been up to while I was supposed to keep his daughter safe. It looked like Evelina could read my thoughts because she began shaking her head menacingly at me.

"Doesn't matter now," Oleg said, brushing off a violent incident. No one screwed Oleg Morozov over without severe repercussions. We were similar in that way, which was why I understood exactly what he'd do to me and why I deserved it. "I've got another flight planned for tomorrow. Sound good?"

I hesitated to answer right away. I was going to be sorry to see her go, and she was also distracting me by waving her hands wildly to be able to tell me something. I asked Oleg to hold on and muted the call, looking at her expectantly.

"Tell him not to come," she said, her eyes wide as she pointed at her screens. She wanted to keep working. It had nothing to do with continuing to spend time with me. "Please, Mikhail," she pleaded. She hurried around the desk and put her arms around me. "I don't want to go home yet."

I pulled back and studied her face. She shook her head, her own eyes steady on mine. She wasn't manipulating me. I leaned down until our foreheads touched. What was I doing? Her father was holding on the phone for me!

"Damn it, Evelina," I said, gently shoving her back to her chair.

She stood by it and stared at me as I picked up my phone again and unmuted Oleg. "It sounds like you've got a lot on your plate," I said, scowling at her as she let out a relieved sigh. "Evelina's perfectly fine here, so why not hold off for now."

"That'd be great," he said. "I know your place out there has better security than anything I've got. It's a big weight off to know she's so safe with you."

"Yep," I said.

"You're a great friend, Mikhail. Let me talk to my baby girl, eh?"

I handed the phone to Evelina, who walked out into the hall to speak to him. She said she was mostly sunning by the pool and not causing any trouble. I could only shake my head at her when she returned. Before I could say a word or even decide what to say, she wrapped her arms around me and kissed me.

"Thank you," she said, shoving away and dancing across the room to get back to work.

I sat with my head in my hands, wondering what I had just done. What the aftermath of all this would be when I stopped living in the moment with Evelina. Because I absolutely had to end things with her. If I was smart, I'd do it before I got in too deep. Which was going to be soon because I almost didn't care what happened to me every time, I saw her smile. That was dangerous and foolish.

The best case scenario was that Oleg never found out, and I lived with the lie between us until I died a natural death many years from now. Worst case? He found out and beat me to a pulp. If I did survive his wrath, Kristina would never speak to me again, which would be worse than dying painfully. I took my head out of my hands and stared at her wistfully. She was already wholly engrossed in her work again.

Well, she didn't have to worry about her father killing her.

She seemed to sense I was staring at her and looked up. Still tapping away, she smiled absently. "You can go; I'm just downloading more data. It'll take a while."

I shook my head, not about to go anywhere, but not for the reason she assumed, based on her sour look.

"I'm not going to cause any trouble by sending anything to anyone. And you know I'm not going to try to escape because I all but begged you to tell Papa not to come for me."

"You did beg," I reminded her, breaking out in a grin as she blushed. "You like begging me, don't you?"

She looked down, trying to hide a smile. "Shut up," she said without any rancor.

A few minutes later, she rubbed her eyes and blinked owlishly. "Enough," I said. "Time to take a break." A glance out the window told me it was an hour or so before sunset. "Let's grab a bottle of wine and take a ride on the airboat," I suggested, cutting off any arguments.

She perked up, agreeing right away, and I was sorry I'd kept her cooped up until now. She ran upstairs to change from the t-shirt and sweats she'd worn to bed and put back on this morning. It turned out I found her just as sexy in the baggy clothes as I did in the skimpy dresses as I watched her bounce up the stairs.

In the kitchen, I took a bottle of white wine from the fridge and put it in a cooler bag. Then I decided I might as well go all in with a picnic and packed an assortment of cheese and lunch meat, adding some crackers and olives for good measure and finally tossing a few brownies the cook had made that day onto the pile. I was searching the pantry for a basket when Evelina found me.

Pulling my head out of the pantry, my jaw dropped at the sight of her in cut-off denim shorts that skimmed her hips and showed almost every inch of her legs. Her ample breasts were barely contained by a red checkered halter top tied behind her neck. Already I imagined pulling on that neat bow so I could stroke her rosy nipples.

"That's a lot of skin," I said, finding a bottle of bug spray and tossing it to her. "You're going to be eaten alive."

She gave me a look that was full of mischievous promise. "I might not mind that so much."

Thankfully she had on practical sneakers, and with the picnic sack slung over my shoulder, we headed out to the airboat dock.

"I didn't see this path when I—" she stopped and searched around for a way to save her slip-up.

"I know you went exploring," I said. "You'd think someone so adept at working with security cameras would have noticed I have them everywhere."

"Oh," she said. "You're not mad?"

"Not anymore. Because you showed good sense in not doing it again."

She grumbled but didn't argue, probably too excited about the prospect of flying over the water in the airboat. After I ensured she was securely strapped in, I couldn't resist showing off a little and sped across the swamp, reveling in her squeals of glee. Her hair was windblown by the time we pulled up to the area I'd had cleared, intending to build a guest house.

I pointed out where everything would eventually be, dismayed at how quickly the Everglades was reclaiming the land. There was still enough space to spread the blanket, and we soon had our picnic meal set out between us. She kept casting the waterline suspicious glances until I assured her most of the time, alligators didn't attack.

"Most of the time," she said distrustfully. "That leaves some of the time. And what about snakes? Or all those giant lizards people import illegally and then dump?"

"I'll wrestle them if they dare to crawl up here," I said.

She knew I was teasing but beamed all the same. We sat out there far too long, watching the birds come home to roost in the nearby trees. We didn't speak about anything consequential, mostly just trading gossip about people we both knew back in Moscow. However, everything she said kept me riveted just because she said it. When I pulled her up to go, she hung back, wanting to drag out our time together as much as I did.

"Fine," I said, pretending to head to the boat without her. "I'll be back to look for your bones tomorrow morning."

Even as she laughed, she hurried to my side, and I wrapped my arms around her. I had to stop this, whatever this was, but not just yet.

"This place is always dangerous, but more so at night," I said, hustling her onto the boat. "We've dawdled too long already." As I jumped up after her, I couldn't help but draw her close again. "You're the most dangerous to me," I said close to her ear.

She shivered. "Don't say that."

I kissed her neck. "It's true, though, Evelina. You know it is."

She held me tight and didn't answer. As the sun dipped lower behind the cypresses, I slowly extricated myself from her hold and motioned for her to buckle up. She still didn't say anything, and we rode back to the house in silence. She knew as well as I did that this had to end. Just not yet.

CHAPTER 15 - EVELINA

If a ruthless crime family didn't have a hit out on me, I would have thought I was living out a perfect dream. The past week was nothing short of incredible.

My project had a few setbacks, mostly due to software glitches that would have taken much less time to fix if Leo had been around. As much as I missed my brother, he would have been a glitch in my dream, keeping me from acting out any fantasy I wanted with Mikhail now that he had finally given up all pretense of trying to resist me. Another annoying inconvenience was not being able to put bugs in the Novikoff's places of business so I could hear as well as see.

When I told Mikhail how I'd used Kristina's many wigs to go around New York and set my listening devices, he'd gone pale, telling me I was lucky I wasn't already fish food in the East River. It was funny how I didn't mind his protectiveness now, but I also had no possible way to do what I normally would have done. If I was currently in New York and he pulled his bossy act, we'd be having some major arguments.

But I wasn't in New York; I was in dreamland.

Ivan and my other cousins had tightened up their security, sending me word through Mikhail that I should sit tight and not worry. I was more than happy to do that, especially with Mikhail hovering around while I worked. He pretended he still didn't trust me, but it was because he couldn't keep his hands off me for long. Another thing that had me bouncing around as if I didn't have a price on my head. The way he was doting on me was the best part of the dream.

Every once in a while over the past few days, I wondered how it could possibly last. Sometimes I tried to play out different scenarios in my mind but usually had to abruptly stop altogether because none of them ended happily. How could they?

In all the years I knew my best friend, I'd never once admitted my true feelings about her father to Kristina. She would have dumped me instantly as a friend or, at the very least, mocked me mercilessly before telling me to knock it the hell off or else.

My father's head would collapse inward from the stress of it, possibly disowning me and very possibly killing Mikhail. Leo would have a fit, which enraged me. As if he'd ever worry as much about my reaction if he got together with Kristina or even her mother if she were still in the picture. Thinking about that made me actually gag.

Okay, so maybe it wasn't so egregious for them to dislike the notion of Mikhail being with me, but what was really so wrong with it? The twenty-year age difference? What were twenty years? I had always been mature for my age, even though my father might teasingly disagree because I was often stubborn. But I knew how to take care of business and had been doing so since I was a teen.

And Mikhail was vibrant and young at heart. His body certainly rivaled any guy my age. Why couldn't we be allowed to fall in love?

I paused with my hands frozen over my keyboard at that thought and shook my head. Of course, we weren't in love. Not really. On my side, I was living out my lifelong fantasy. On his side… who knew? But it wasn't love.

It would be nice, though. Really nice.

No, I couldn't think that way, or I'd start to want that. A life with Mikhail where we made decisions, picked out furniture, planned vacations, chose baby names…

Never going to happen, and to dwell on it was a one-way ticket to a broken heart that surely wouldn't mend. My crush on him had caused me a great deal of pain over the years already, but if I let myself believe I was in love with him, we had a chance at all the things I liked to daydream about? It would be better to turn myself over to the Novikoffs than face that kind of pain.

I pushed it all aside and tried to concentrate on debugging the few lines of code I was trying to implement into Leo's program. A big commotion in the hall made me look up to see several unobtrusive but always hovering guards rush past my open office door. Curious and a bit frightened of what had them flapping from their roosts, I hurried to follow them down the stairs and outside.

I stayed in the front doorway, watching as they congregated in the courtyard. Everyone was looking up and several of them aimed guns at the sky. It was then I noticed a mechanical humming and followed their gazes to see a drone quite a ways up and still in the distance, but heading in the direction of the house.

Mikhail stood in the center of the guards, giving them orders I couldn't make out. He turned to notice me in that way he had, always sensing when I was around.

"Get inside," he shouted, taking a step toward me. "Go upstairs and lock yourself in, and don't come out until I get you."

His tone and look weren't to be argued with, and I turned around to obey his orders. Before I got in the house, I heard the crack of a gun and whirled back to see one of the guards had shot the drone. I watched it spiral downward toward the courtyard as Mikhail barked orders about how to deal with it when it hit the ground. If he saw me still hanging around in the doorway when that happened, there'd be hell to pay.

Despite my fear for his safety, I turned and fled up the stairs, telling myself no one was more capable than Mikhail. He'd be fine. I took the stairs two at a time and barreled into his suite. There was a safe room behind his walk-in closet that he'd shown me in case of an emergency, and that was where he'd meant for me to lock myself into.

I didn't like the idea of being shut in that tiny room without knowing what was happening, so I locked myself in his room, leaning against the door and straining to listen. His room was on the back side of the house, so looking out the windows was useless. Holding my breath, I waited for an explosion, a crash, more shouting. None came. All was quiet. That didn't necessarily mean safety, though. If poison gas was released from the drone, that was sure to be silent.

Yes, he was capable and surrounded by armed guards. But that would be little help if that drone held any of the terrible things that rushed through my imagination after I thought of poison gas. Letting my breath out in a rush, I began to pace. A few minutes passed, growing to ten, then fifteen. I couldn't handle not knowing in that eerie silence and unlocked the door. Opening it a crack and peeking my head around revealed an empty hallway.

I crept out and tiptoed down the hall, poking my head through every open door, trying to find Mikhail or anyone who could tell me what was happening. There was no sign of anyone, and that, combined with the dead quiet, unnerved me enough to quit creeping on my toes and pick up my pace.

I finally found him in his main office, just down the hall from mine. He sat at his desk, surrounded by his guards, all of them staring intently at his computer screen. The distress on their faces made my stomach drop. Something was clearly wrong. But what danger could come from a screen? I took a step into the room, and Mikhail's head shot up. His face was stricken and pale, making my stomach sink lower.

"Get back upstairs," he ordered, meeting my eye with a pleading look in his. "Go now, Evelina."

The look on his face made me want to listen to him. With all my being, I didn't want to see what had all those big strong men so upset. But something kept me moving forward toward his desk. Something told me I had to know what they were looking at, even though I dreaded it.

CHAPTER 16 - MIKHAIL

I stood in the kitchen with the cook, who was helping me prepare a romantic surprise for Evelina. Since she had enjoyed the impromptu picnic in the secluded clearing so much, I decided to put a little more effort into another one. This time I meant to take her somewhere closer to the house. Still private, but less chance of a snake sliding across our legs if we got frisky after the meal.

The cook had found a big wicker basket and had filled it with wine glasses and silverware. No more eating with our fingers or swigging straight from the bottle this time. I was being so serious about this occasion even though every day when I woke up with her body entwined with mine, I knew I had to put a stop to things. And every day, I decided to let it go a little longer.

We were discussing what food to pack when my phone interrupted us. Seeing that one of my security team patrolled the wall, I answered it right away. As well-defended as the place was, I never totally let my guard down.

"Boss, I've got a sighting of a drone heading your way. Should I take it out?"

I went on high alert, trying to convince myself it was someone making a documentary about the Everglades and gathering footage.

"Negative," I said. "Let's wait and see if it passes overhead."

Still, I called the house guards to head outside in case more was incoming than a drone. They jumped at the chance to finally do something, and I followed them out into the courtyard to wait and see what happened. We all stood around, craning our necks as it buzzed into view. There was no way Evelina didn't notice all that commotion, and when I turned around, she stood in the front doorway.

Terror that she might get caught on the drone's camera made me holler at her to get inside. So far, I was positive no one from the Novikoff family knew she was here. All I needed was for them to get their confirmation and launch a full offensive against my fortress to get to her. She seemed to sense how serious I was and turned tail and fled inside.

Only then could I look back up at the drone, which was now directly overhead and losing altitude.

"Take it out," I told the nearest man with a gun.

In one shot, the small machine came plummeting to the earth, landing with an anticlimactic thump. White dust rose in every direction as it scattered the crushed shells of the courtyard. All of my armed guys aimed their guns at it, but it only lay there in a broken heap of plastic and wires. We waited a minute, but nothing happened. I approached it warily, turning to shrug at the guards.

"It's just a delivery drone," I said.

That might have been fine, except I would never have allowed anything to come in this way, even if I had ordered something recently. Everything we got on the island was left at a drop point in the closest town, fifteen miles away. Someone would retrieve it and drive it in, going through the same security checkpoints as anyone who made it this far.

I leaned over the shattered drone and kicked it. Still, nothing happened, but when it rolled onto its side, I saw the small package attached to it. Barely larger than a deck of cards and wrapped in plain brown paper with no markings that I could see.

"Let me grab it," one of my guys said, but I waved him back.

They went above and beyond for me, and I was almost sure this wasn't anything to panic over, but I wasn't completely sure. I tugged it from its cable and turned it over in my hands. It weighed next to nothing, but there was writing on the other side. One word.

Watch.

Okay, not too cryptic. I gave it a tentative shake, and when we still weren't blown to smithereens, I tore the paper off and opened the box.

Inside was a rectangular silver USB stick wrapped in bubble wrap. No other note, nothing.

"I guess we watch it," I said, heading back inside.

In my office, I flipped off the cap, still half expecting an explosion of some kind. It seemed to really just be a plain old USB stick.

"Hang on," Andre said, muscling past the others before I could put it in one of the slots on my computer. "There might be a virus on it. Let me just…" He sat in my chair, clicking on things in rapid succession, then leaned under the desk and pulled out a few cords. "Now it's not connected to anything. It might wreck this machine, but it won't be able to travel to the network."

"Good job," I said, impressed. He'd been out of sight since Evelina continued to hold a grudge against him for his part in her abduction, but he was one of my best.

I plugged it in, waiting to see what was on there. My stomach twisted into a knot when I saw a lone video file pop up on the screen. I reached for my phone as my hand hovered over the mouse, tapping the first number in my contacts before I played the video.

Kristina answered right away, letting me breathe again. "Hey, I'm just about to go into an audition—"

"Sorry, sweetie," I interrupted, clicking on the video file now that I knew my daughter wasn't going to be on it. What loaded up on the screen sickened me almost as much as what my imagination had conjured. "It was just a mistake, but I'd love to talk to you later."

I ended the call, not taking my eyes off the horrific video unfolding before me, surprised I could make my voice sound so normal and pleasant.

"Jesus," I muttered. Movement in the doorway made me drag my eyes from the scene to see Evelina standing in the doorway. My heart lurched. I couldn't let her see this. "Get back upstairs," I shouted, too angrily. I could tell she knew something was wrong immediately and approached the desk. "Go now, Evelina."

Her eyes were locked with mine, full of fear as she seemed to read what I was thinking. But she couldn't know, and I couldn't let her. As she picked up her pace and hurried around my desk, I fumbled for the mouse to shut the video down. I was too slow, and she put her hand over mine to stop me, leaning over my shoulder to peer at the screen.

"No," she whimpered, her voice cracking. "No, please, no."

Her brother Leo was her other half, maybe the only person she completely trusted in the world. Nearly inseparable, he was always within shouting distance when they were apart. One time she was at our house having a sleepover with Kristina. She had woken up in the middle of the night, hysterically demanding to be taken home. At the same time, Leo was being rushed to the hospital with appendicitis. Somehow she knew.

My daughter may have been her best friend, but her twin was on another level entirely.

And now she had to watch him being ruthlessly beaten on the video. He was bound to a chair in an empty room. His face was already battered and bruised, with blood streaming from his nose and over his split lips. One eye was completely swollen shut. Despite his state, he was still awake as a man whose back was turned to the camera continued to pummel him with his fists. Again and again, each meaty whack made Evelina draw in a sharp sob. The unidentified assailant only stopped throwing punches when Leo slumped forward in the chair he was shackled to, entirely still.

Evelina cried out and leaned closer as if she couldn't believe what she saw. Tears streamed down her pale face, and I realized she had my hand in a death grip. She held her breath as she stared unblinking at her brother. It had been a long time since I prayed, but I silently offered up a plea that she wouldn't have to suffer such heartache. Leo's chest finally rose a half second before the video ended, and everyone in the room breathed a sigh of relief. Evelina let go of my hand and sank to the floor, staring up at me with hollow eyes.

"I'll get him back," I said, kneeling beside her. "I promise I'll get him back safe and sound."

I would have promised her anything if only I could erase the hopeless look on her face.

Chapter 17 - Evelina

It wasn't real. It couldn't be real. Seeing Leo being savagely beaten—my fault, all my fault—broke something inside me. Not my big, burly genius of a brother who was always quick with a joke and quicker with his fists, who could cleanly shoot a cap off a bottle at a hundred paces. Who always stuck by me, no matter what nonsense I wanted to get up to. The only thing he wouldn't do was let me put myself in danger.

It was like I could feel every punch as it landed. It should have been me. It was all my fault.

The next thing I knew, I was on the floor, with Mikhail kneeling beside me, saying something I couldn't register at first. My brain felt like it was full of swarming bees, the horror of what I saw drowning everything else out. I felt his hand on my back, and finally, his firm voice broke through.

"I'll get him back. I promise I'll get him back safe and sound."

I wanted to believe him. I had to. The thought of never seeing Leo again threatened to keep me on the floor forever, but I clung to Mikhail's promise. My legs felt like they were in deep quicksand, but my thoughts were becoming clearer. My brother was in trouble. He needed me.

If the situation were reversed, Leo would have already leaped into action. He wouldn't be huddling in a puddle on the floor. I wiped away the tears I didn't realize had been flowing down my cheeks. Shaking but getting stronger by the second, I dragged myself to my feet.

At some point when I'd been sniveling, Mikhail must have dismissed his guards. We were alone in his office. The terrible video was still loaded on his computer screen, and that final frame of Leo passed out in the chair those monsters had tied him to, still visible.

Mikhail noticed I was transfixed by it and turned the monitor off with a curse.

"I'll get him back," he said again.

"How?" I asked.

His eyes skated away from mine. I believed he wanted to help and would do everything in his power to save Leo, but I could tell he didn't know how to start yet.

"You should stay out of it," he told me.

I would have laughed if I hadn't just seen something that stole a piece of my soul. "You better not try to leave me out of it, Mikhail."

His eyes narrowed, and he pressed his lips together. To hell with it. I didn't have time to argue with him. My legs had regained their strength. I turned and stalked away. He grabbed my hand before I reached the door.

"Where are you going?" He wasn't being harsh. His voice sounded pained as if he hated not knowing what to do.

"I'm going to find a gun and shoot you if you don't let me help save Leo."

He raked his fingers through his hair, looking like a frustrated porcupine by the time he stopped. One hand was still wrapped around mine.

"The Novikoffs must know you're here now," he started slowly. It wasn't a direct admonishment, but it felt like a slap in my guilt-ridden state. But while I had started this, it wasn't about me now. I nodded tersely for him to continue. He closed his eyes. "Since there's no way they can breach the island, they're trying to flush you out, don't you see? They want you where you'll be more vulnerable."

He was right. Furious tears welled in my eyes, and I crammed my fists into the sockets to keep them from falling. "I don't care," I croaked around my clogged throat. "Mikhail, he's my brother."

He pulled me into his arms. I couldn't fight him and didn't want to. His comforting hands rubbing my back kept me from falling to pieces. I struggled to find the words to explain to him how much I needed to help. Logic told me my presence would probably make no difference, but my heart had to be where Leo was.

"Okay," Mikhail said, his chin resting on the top of my head.

I jerked back to look up at him, shocked he had agreed. But I could see in his eyes he understood somehow, and I melted against him with relief and gratitude.

"But only if you listen to every word I say and do every last thing I tell you," he added. "If anything starts to go south, you're out, got it?"

I nodded against his chest. "Yes, I've got it." I held on tight. Of course, Mikhail understood. "Thank you."

Invigorated by fresh purpose, I pushed away from his warm embrace and hurried back to his computer, snatching out the USB stick and heading to my own office.

"What are you doing?" He followed me down the hall.

I prayed my hunch was correct. "They're idiots, remember? They never checked all their camera feeds after they figured out I hacked them." I flew into my office and sat down, flicking my sleeping screens to life. "Maybe," I said, inserting the USB into a port. "Just maybe somebody slipped up somewhere."

I opened the metadata on the file, trying to keep my hopes level as I scanned the information. Mikhail sat across from me, his hands planted on the desk as he leaned over, trying to see what I was doing. My heavy heart grew lighter as I found what I sought and whooped in triumph.

"What's going on? What did you find?" he asked, rushing around to crouch beside me. He stared at the screen, which was probably gibberish to him, but was as good as a map to me.

I jabbed at the metadata and then switched tabs to pull up a map. "Whoever sent this was either impatient, sloppy or just plain stupid. Maybe all three. They never wiped the location information. A fifth grader should know to do something like that before sending out pictures or videos."

He grimaced. "I wouldn't know how to do that."

I smiled, my face feeling rickety and out of practice. This was good news, but Leo still wasn't safe. "God, I love you, old boomers," I said. "You make my life so much easier."

He let the mild insult roll off his shoulders. "So you know where he is?"

The smile disappeared. "Kind of." I pointed to the map. "He's in North Miami, but the exact location isn't super accurate." Zooming in on the street view, the coordinates I'd pulled from the file showed a deserted

104

parking lot. "It's a start. Leo will be nearby. There's a bunch of buildings in this area."

One of them might contain the bare, concrete room where he was being held. Or, had been held. The date on the video was from a day prior. The weight settled back on my heart, threatening to sink me in despair. A lot could happen in a day.

Mikhail squeezed my shoulder bracingly. "Get ready to leave. We'll head to that location right away."

I raced upstairs to change into something suitable for a fight. It took me less than three minutes to tear off the sundress and put on my old jeans and one of my new oversized t-shirts. Andre, the mountain-sized security guard who first jumped me in the park, waited outside my room. He handed me a kevlar vest and a computer tablet.

"From the boss," he grunted, falling into step beside me down the stairs.

"No gun?" I asked.

He only grunted again, his face an emotionless brick as he turned to me. "My orders are to keep you safe and help get your brother back in that order. You gonna make either of those things difficult for me?"

I shook my head and hugged the vest close to my chest. This big brute still gave me the creeps, but he was definitely capable and would be an asset in the rescue mission. "Thank you," I all but choked out.

He could have smirked, but his face remained impassive. At the front door, he veered off to get in the first of three dark SUVs. Mikhail waited by the middle one; the third was already running, ready to go as soon as the order was given. I ran to his side, and he opened the back door for me to get in.

Once he was seated beside me, he gave the order, and the small convoy moved out, heading down the long route to get off the island and make its way up north. I kept a firm grip on my new tablet and the kevlar vest, holding them close like security blankets.

"You can see the location on that," Mikhail said, tapping the tablet. "I thought you might like to know where we were and how close we were getting. The vest is probably self-explanatory. When we get there, I'll assess your need for a firearm. Or if you leave the car at all."

I nodded, too grateful he was taking charge of the operation to argue. The fear I struggled to keep at bay began to creep back in. Now that we were on our way, I could only stare at the map. Dark thoughts of what we might find when we arrived made it difficult to breathe.

What if we were too late?

Chapter 18 - Mikhail

In the car, Evelina remained silent and huddled close to me, her eyes glued to the map on the tablet I gave her, hoping to keep her from obsessing about what we might find. Now it seemed like a bad idea as she only stared morosely at the blue dot on the screen, her knuckles white as she held it in a vice grip.

I worried she might be in shock, so I closely watched her. Once we got off my island, the trip would take a little more than an hour, which wasn't long in a normal situation, but it could seem like days to someone sunk in despair. I wished I could make more promises, but I didn't dare. Not when I wasn't sure I could keep them.

The Novikoffs had done a real number on Leo, which was only the portion they'd recorded to taunt us. I tried not to, but I feared the worst, and it was tearing me up not being able to offer Evelina any real comfort.

Another task I didn't want to face was calling Oleg to keep him informed and assure him I was doing everything I could. With a sigh, I pulled my phone from my pocket and scrolled to his number, my thumb hovering over the call button.

Before I could tap it, Evelina slapped the phone out of my hand and dove for it when it hit the floor at my feet. Once she made sure the call hadn't gone through, she turned to me with fire in her eyes.

"What in the hell are you doing? Trying to give an old man a heart attack?"

"Your father is only ten years older than me," I said. It shouldn't have stung at a time like that, and if things with Leo hadn't been so dire, it might have been an awkward situation.

"I still don't want you worrying him." She held the phone in both hands, tight to her chest, as she glared at me.

"He has a right to know," I argued. "I'd want to know if Kristina was in trouble."

Her face turned red, then slowly eased back to normal. She handed over my phone. "Put it on speaker so I can talk to him too."

I did as she asked, pleased a bit of her spark had returned. But as soon as Oleg was on the phone, she talked over me, downplaying everything.

"Hi, Papa," she called out with forced merriment as she glared at me. "Leo's got himself in a little bit of trouble, but Mikhail and I are taking care of it."

"A little bit of trouble?" I hissed. She swatted my leg.

"Ah, I'm glad you and Mikhail are getting along," Oleg said.

Some pink returned to her cheeks, and she dropped her gaze from mine. "Yes, he's treating me well, Papa. You don't need to worry about that. You don't have to worry about anything."

I was shocked at how she babied him, lying to protect his feelings. Did Kristina do the same thing to me? I wondered if every time she told me something was fine or even great, it was all lies.

"I'm going to make sure Leo's safe," I said weakly, hating every second of the ruse.

"Should I come to Miami after all?" Oleg asked, sounding worried.

"Don't bother yourself," Evelina said. "We're heading to pick up Leo now. Everything's *fine*."

Surely he wouldn't believe her? "Good, good, darling. Keep me updated."

"Of course, Papa."

"And Mikhail?" he said. "Thanks for watching over my babies."

I had no answer for that. How was I watching over them? I was sleeping with one, and the other was currently in mortal danger. I wasn't the only one who looked uncomfortable about his outpouring of gratitude. Evelina ended the call and stared straight ahead with pursed lips.

"He didn't mean anything," I said. "Parents always think of their kids as babies. He knows you're an adult. I still think of Kristina as a little kid most of the time, too." I had tried defending my old friend but realized I had only put my foot in my mouth. Evelina and my daughter were the same age, for God's sake. Now was not the time to recognize for the hundredth time that I needed to end things with her. Not until we found Leo.

"Wow," she said, shaking her head at me.

I changed tack, anything to get her off the age issue. "So what's with all the lying to your father? Is that a regular thing with you?" I couldn't help myself. I had to know. "Does Kristina do that to me, too?

She handed back my phone with a smug look. I supposed it was better than the sickly fear, but it was still galling. "Of course she does. We do it to protect you."

"Wow," I said, repeating her own sentiment. I was utterly appalled.

She shrugged. "There's no reason for him to make himself sick when there's nothing he can do. If—" she stopped and took a shaky breath. "If he needs to know something, we'll tell him then."

"Fine," I said. "I guess that makes sense." It still rankled, though.

She was clearly over-talking about her father and no longer thinking about the age gap between us anymore because she clenched her fists and leaned forward. "Can't he drive faster?"

"We're already going as fast as we can without drawing attention. Either from law enforcement or anyone who might be tailing us."

The fear rushed back into her face. "Do you think someone is?"

"Better to be safe than sorry."

In fact, my paranoia that someone might have been lying in wait for her to leave the island, I had our convoy pull into a hotel twenty minutes later, where I had arranged to have a different car waiting for me. When no one followed us into the garage, and Andre said no one seemed to be suspicious out on the street, Evelina and I continued in the new car. The other two left ahead of us and went in separate directions, prepared to take a different route and meet up with us at the location.

I wanted to wait a little longer, keeping eyes on the road beneath us from our spot in the parking garage. The traffic moved along at a normal pace. No one was in any of the parked cars, and no one else entered the garage while we were there.

"We're wasting time," Evelina snapped, pacing back and forth beside our car while the driver kept a lookout with me.

I nodded to the driver, who got in the car, then I took Evelina in my arms. "Everything will be fine."

She rested her head against my chest and sighed, too frazzled to argue, which broke my heart a little. I pulled away, overwhelmed by the confused mix of feelings I had for her. None of it was right, at least not now. I needed to be ready at the drop of a hat to commit violence if we found the people who took Leo and caused her so much worry and pain. That meant I needed to stay focused. And not on comforting Evelina, as much as I might have wanted to.

"We'll be there very soon," I said, tucking her into the backseat.

I had to be mentally prepared for whatever came next, not wrapped up in emotions. I closed the back door and got in front with the driver, blocking out her look of hurt and trying to ignore the searing pain of feeling like I was abandoning her.

CHAPTER 19 - EVELINA

It was no time to feel bad about Mikhail when I was already eaten up with worry over Leo. But why was he suddenly pulling away? I blamed the phone call to my father, dragging him back to reality. I also hated that it seemed like he still lumped me in with Kristina, making out that there was an us versus them, kids versus grown-ups mentality with us just because I didn't want my father to end up in the hospital on top of everything else.

Would I ever be completely, one hundred percent honest with my father? It was laughable as if he'd never lied to me. And certainly not in a malicious way to hurt me. My father loved me more than his own life, but I wasn't stupid. There were probably dozens of times he'd wanted to spare me hurt feelings or keep me out of harm's way with a bending of the truth. As I was certain Mikhail had done for Kristina over the years.

He was being willfully pigheaded if he couldn't see it was exactly the same when we did it for them. And he was being foolish if he cared about our age difference, too. I certainly didn't.

The map indicated we were very close, and tension built up in me as I watched the city pass by outside the new SUV's tinted windows. At first, I'd been annoyed at his overly cautious waste of time, but when I thought about the video and what the Novikoffs were capable of doing to get their hands on me, I was relieved for the extra layer of security.

I still practically bounced in my seat with pent-up nerves. When the driver and Mikhail were watching the street from the parking garage, I snuck one of the guns from the arsenal into the front seat. A small handgun that fit nicely in the waistband of my jeans and could be easily covered with my oversized t-shirt. Hopefully, they wouldn't notice it was missing because I refused to be unarmed.

If I saw anyone who had something to do with Leo's torture, it was going to be me who put the bullet in them.

I stopped looking out the window when we moved into more deserted territory and concentrated on the map. When we arrived, I looked out to see the same parking lot from the street view map, and it was still completely empty. The two other cars in our original convoy pulled up a moment later. It was time. I pulled on the kevlar vest and got out before Mikhail could order me to stay put, turning in a circle to assess the area.

The parking lot was smaller than it appeared, only about ten spots, the yellow lines almost completely faded, and the asphalt cracked and pitted. It had been unused for quite a while by the clearly abandoned office complex it was attached to. The brick building was much longer than it was tall, taking up half the block and three stories high. It might have been one of the old cigar factories, but then modernized and converted to offices. Based on the sagging, padlocked doors, and mostly boarded-up windows, it probably hadn't seen any legitimate business in at least ten years.

The place was one of many in a long row of industrial buildings, half abandoned. The few companies that seemed to be hanging on by a thread in the sorry place were closed since it was after five. But I took note of two cameras that might still be working and might come in handy if Leo wasn't here.

Please let him be here and be okay.

Mikhail got out and did the same slow sweep I did, nodding curtly to me. "Stay with the driver," he said, moving closer to the chained and locked front door.

The driver got out and pulled out his gun, standing at attention at the front of the car. I pulled out my own pilfered gun and hurried to catch up with Mikhail.

"I'm not staying back," I said, meeting him at the door.

He noticed my piece right away but only raised an eyebrow. "You think you're faster than me with that thing?"

I lowered the gun to my side, pointing it at the ground. With my free hand, I grabbed a handful of his shirt and stood on my toes to get right in his face. "You will have to kill me to keep me from going in there."

He rolled his eyes and sighed. "No, I won't. Don't be ridiculous, Evelina. You agreed to do what I said."

Frustration made me huff like a bull being taunted with a red cape. "Then I will make you pay until the end of your life if you don't let me."

Then I realized I didn't need his permission. He might have been in charge of me years ago when I was at Kristina's house, and he was the only adult around. But I was an adult now. He knew it, too.

"Go ahead and shoot me if you want to, Mikhail," I said, slamming the butt of my gun down on the old, rusty padlock. With a crack, it fell open, and I slipped it off the chain. "I'm going in."

I heard him release a string of swear words, but he soon fell into step beside me. I didn't grin at him triumphantly, and he didn't scowl at me. We had a job to do. He did a quick sweep of the big lobby, empty except for an ancient desk that listed to one side on only three legs and an accumulation of broken liquor bottles lining the stained walls. And the stink. It reeked of stale beer and piss, and I struggled not to gag.

The place was so old it still had the kind of elevator that you had to pull the cage door down and was cobwebbed over and growing moss inside. I opened the emergency stairwell door, and he poked his head around it, quickly ducking back out. The smell in there was worse than the lobby, wafting out after him.

"There are some offices down that hall," he said. "Start there, you think?"

We looked into the first one. It was too small and too bright, with the late afternoon sun spilling through the broken window. The next office's window was boarded up, but it was still too bright, and the walls were cheap, moldy paneling. The room Leo had been in had plain cement block walls.

"I don't think it's any of the offices," I said, starting to feel defeated.

Location data on images was often inaccurate, and while I knew we were in the right general area, there were still lots of other buildings around. Every minute that passed was time that Leo wasn't getting the help he needed. On the other side of the lobby was a metal door with fresh handprints in the thick layer of dust.

"Look at this," I said, perking up as I hurried to open it.

Mikhail hissed and jumped in front of me. "Will you be careful? There could have been an ambush."

I steadied my patience and let him look before me, then he nodded the all-clear. There were more stairs, but this time leading down.

"Buildings in Florida don't usually have basements, do they?" I asked.

He nodded. "It would be awfully convenient to find one that did, though." He took my wrist and gave me a stern look. "I'll go down first. Don't follow until I tell you it's okay."

I nodded and waited until he was three steps ahead of me before following, ignoring his sigh. When this was all over, I would explain I wasn't trying to be stubborn or flout his orders. I understood he was concerned for my safety, but I was only thinking about my brother when we might be close enough to free him. Fear of what might be waiting down there threatened to suffocate me, but Leo had to be all right, didn't he? Surely I would feel it if he wasn't.

Once we were halfway down, the stairwell was almost pitch black, with barely any light from above filtering down and obviously no windows below. Mikhail pulled out his phone and turned on the flashlight, casting a spooky glow on a dusty concrete floor. He stopped at the bottom and waited for me to catch up, keeping me from moving past him.

It was huge down there, probably as long and wide as the entire building, and his light only showed a small portion of it. There was a gloomy air of desperation about the place; the only positive was that it smelled slightly less awful than the lobby. More mold and damp than anything else. He cast the beam at the walls, and I sucked in a breath.

"The same cement blocks," I said, trying to brush past him. "He's here. He has to be."

He wrapped his arm around my waist to keep me from moving forward. "Just hold on and be quiet."

We waited for a breathless second, listening for any slight sound, but everything was silent. Not even the scuttle of a cockroach or rat.

"No one's here," he said.

"He could be unconscious." I broke free and hurried forward into the dark corners of the basement.

With yet another sigh, Mikhail followed me, flashing the light in all directions but only showing bare walls and dusty floors.

"Leo?" I called in a low voice, then again a bit louder. His name echoed back to me, but it seemed like Mikhail was right.

"Look," he said, a few feet away from me.

He cast the light to the floor to reflect off a damp stain. The entire place had various damp stains, but this one chilled me to the bone. Blood, not old and dried up. Freshly spilled. As he moved the beam of light along the floor, I could see it was an alarmingly large stain.

"He was here," I said. "But where is he now?"

His flashlight beam continued to dance along the floor, and he swept it back and forth, seeming to follow something. "There are spatters," he said. "Leading this way. Damn it, this place is so filthy we didn't notice."

He took my hand and tugged me back toward the stairs, taking them two at a time. We had to shield our eyes from the blast of brightness at the top, but after a second, he leaned over, ambling and looking for more of a trail.

"There's none by the front door," Mikhail said, moving slowly down the hall, back toward the offices.

I followed suit and began peering carefully at the floor in the main lobby and found a few drops by the emergency stairwell leading up. I shouted excitedly, and he came running.

"The stairs might be dangerous," he said, not a lick of hope in his eyes that I would volunteer to return to the parking lot with the guards.

"Let's be careful, then," I said, heading into the stairwell.

The stairs were sturdy, just crowded with litter. Empty cans and smashed bottles, moldy fast food wrappers, and cigarette butts were the only things inhibiting our ascent. None of it looked recent. Even the squatters had long given up on this derelict building, making it the perfect spot to indulge in a bit of torture. Or hide... No, I wasn't thinking like that. I'd become paralyzed if I thought that way.

Every few feet, one of us spotted more blood drops, so we kept moving up. On the third floor, another short stairway led to the roof. Pausing at the metal door, Mikhail pulled out his gun. Then we both jumped when his phone rang. He swore, pulling it out to silence it.

"It's Andre," he said, answering it. "What?" After a short pause, while he listened, his eyes grew round. "What!? Yes, we're at the roof level now. Jesus Christ."

It was killing me only hearing half of the conversation, and the look on his face as he listened to whatever his guard told him didn't bode well. He ended the call and gave me a long look.

"There's something on the roof," he said.

"Yeah, no shit."

He shook his head. "You need to get back downstairs and stay with the men."

I tried to push past him, panic fueling me to get through that door. "No way," I said, my voice coming out a squeak.

He gripped my shoulders. "Evelina, let me take care of this. You need to use your head right now, not your heart."

For a flash, I wondered if this was why he pulled away from me on the drive over. I had to get my mind right, stop being a mess of emotions. "You can go first, but I'm not going back downstairs."

"Get your gun up and stay behind me," he ordered, all business as he turned to crack open the door.

No one jumped him, so he pushed it open far enough to get through. I followed, and having seen a movie or two in my lifetime, I propped open the roof access door with one of the many bottles lying everywhere so we wouldn't be stuck up there.

"Fuck," he muttered as soon as he was around the door.

Fear kept me rooted to the spot, but only for a blink. Then I moved to his side. "Leo," I shrieked, making Mikhail slap his hand over my mouth, the other around my middle to keep me from leaping forward.

Leo was still in the chair from the video, still slumped over. Unconscious, only unconscious. But the chair was at the very edge of the building, teetering over the side in a bizarre, alarming manner, seeming to defy gravity. I struggled to get free to race over and jerk my brother back to safety. The building wasn't a highrise, but a thirty-foot drop in his condition would end him.

"Stay here," Mikhail said. Didn't he get tired of it? "I'll get him. If anything happens, get the hell downstairs. Do not try to help me, understand?"

116

I couldn't take my eyes off the way the chair wobbled at the edge, as if I could keep it from falling over with the sheer force of my mind. I let Mikhail move slowly closer to Leo, determined to stay put and keep using my invisible twin powers to keep him safe. But I couldn't stand the suspense and scrambled after him.

Up close, I could see that the psychopaths had tied the chair to a rope connected to an old air conditioning unit near the stairwell. The rope scraped over a rough concrete block so that it began to fray every time Leo moved or the chair shifted. It was already halfway to snapping. I had never been so glad to see my brother unconscious because any more struggling to free himself would have been his certain demise.

Mikhail got to him before me, reaching for Leo when there was a scuffle behind me. Whirling around, I saw two armed men emerging from behind the stairwell, looking more shocked to see me than I was them.

Their surprise and a single second of hesitation saved my life. I had my gun at the ready, and before the first one could get a hand on his, I shouted to warn Mikhail. At the same time, I squeezed the trigger. The first one dropped with a neat hole through his forehead, and I turned my gun on the second, but Mikhail had already turned and laid him out with a shot through the chest. He stomped over, put another slug in his head to make sure, and then faced me.

"We have to work fast. There might be others in the area who heard the shots."

We dragged Leo back from the edge, and Mikhail whipped out a knife to cut away the thick ropes and zip ties that bound him. My brother must have put up a hell of a fight to warrant all that. I fervently hoped he broke some bones before they got the better of him, the damn cowards.

I gently patted his battered cheeks, and he groaned but didn't open his eyes. It was enough, for now, to know he was alive, but he was in terrible shape. With some effort, Mikhail hoisted him over his shoulder and carried him down the stairs. I followed, trying to make sure his head didn't get jostled too much, but Mikhail was in a hurry.

The sound of gunshots greeted us just as I was about to open the front door, and we dropped down. As Mikhail laid Leo on the ground and readied his gun, I peeked out over the edge of a window. The three SUVs were parked in a line. Mikhail's men were all hunkered down behind them, intermittently rising up to fire off a shot. Still, they were pinned in their position since the other shooters had higher ground.

"Two on the roof across from us," I said, dropping below the window. "My gun doesn't have the range, and I'm not sure I can make that shot with yours," I said.

Mikhail crawled over and had a look for himself. "I might be able to get one of them, but it's fifty-fifty, and even if I did, it'd alert the other to our position."

From behind us, I heard a familiar groan and whipped around to see Leo raise his bloody face. "Give me the gun," he said, his split, swollen lips curling into a grin as best he could. "God, my face hurts. Actually, everything hurts."

I crawled to his side and grabbed his hand. "You look like shit, too," I said, my eyes filling with tears.

With a Herculean effort, he sat up with another pained groan. "Quit acting like a baby," he said, weakly squeezing my hand. He blinked a few times in Mikhail's direction before recognizing him. "Oh, hey, Mikhail. It's been a long time."

"Lie back down and save your strength," he told him. "We can catch up later when my guys get us out of here."

With heaving breaths, Leo dragged himself to the window and looked out. "They're not getting a shot. I can do it. Give me your gun."

"We already discussed this," Mikhail said. "I could probably take one out, but it would give away our position. I won't risk them knowing your sister is here."

Leo closed his eyes, and I thought he might have slipped back into unconsciousness again, but he was only gathering strength. "You *might* be able to get one, but I *can* get both. Nobody's fucking with Evelina today."

I beamed at him, then reached for Mikhail's gun. "Nobody can shoot like Leo," I said proudly. "If he says he can get them, he'll get them."

"Your shoulder's clearly broken, and your eye is swollen shut," Mikhail argued.

I kept holding out my hand. "He can do it with no shoulders and no eyes."

Leo laughed, then groaned at the pain. "I don't remember the last time I ate, and I'm in a lot of fucking pain," he said, all seriousness now. "Give me the gun."

I wriggled it from Mikhail's grasp and handed it over, then asked Leo if he needed any help. He took a few moments to decide on the right place to take aim, and Mikhail helped him move over a couple feet. I knelt behind him to steady him if the recoil knocked him back into his weakened state, even though he told me I was being silly.

"I think you're drawing things out for dramatic effect," I said. "Go ahead and finish this if you're so hungry."

And just like that, with two rapid-fire and expertly aimed shots, the snipers were neutralized. He slipped back below the window, all his teasing and bravado spent. He gave me another lopsided smile before closing his eyes.

"He's out again," I said, making sure his pulse was still strong.

"I'll be damned," Mikhail said. "He actually did it."

A few moments later, Andre shouted the all-clear, and Mikhail took Leo under the shoulders, deciding he could be dragged the last few yards to the car. "He's as big as I am," he said when I indignantly disagreed with him.

Andre came in and helped carry him more gently, and I kept my gun up the last few steps to the car in case anyone else popped out. Once they had him sprawled across the third-row backseat, I scrambled in after him, almost expecting Mikhail to ride up front again.

But he got in next to me, and the driver closed the door before trotting around to get us moving again. I reached for his hand and tried to say everything I felt, but I could only smile at him and hold on. He had not only saved me from the Novikoffs, though it took me a bit to realize that was what he was doing, he'd also saved Leo.

My heart welled up with gratitude and relief, and I peeked over to make sure Leo was still out before planting a kiss on his lips. He returned the kiss, slow and gentle, before letting his head drop back against the seat, his eyes closed.

"We'll be at a safe house of mine soon," he said. "I'm just going to take a little rest. You Morozovs wear me the hell out."

"You earned a nap," I said, squeezing his hand.

By the time we were back on the highway, he was asleep. If only everything was right with the world, but Leo was badly injured and not out of the woods despite his courageous display. He looked so ragged and pitiful that I let go of Mikhail's hand and climbed into the back to make sure he didn't roll off onto the floor and hurt himself worse.

I was overjoyed to have Leo back, but I couldn't help but wonder if this marked the end of my dream time with Mikhail.

CHAPTER 20 - MIKHAIL

I woke up with a start as the car pulled down the winding drive to the small cottage in Hialeah that I kept for emergencies. The faded pink stucco facade wasn't much to look at. Still, it was always well stocked with food and medical supplies. The birds of paradise and hibiscus were in full bloom, making it seem more welcoming and homier.

I reached for Evelina's hand, but she had moved to the backseat to stare at her brother. It was like she thought she could keep him alive if she never took her eyes off of him. I had to admit I'd had similar feelings when Kristina was a baby, and I was always worried when she was out of my sight. I didn't begrudge Evelina's love for her twin, but it did seem that now that he was with us, it had to finally mark the end of our little… whatever it was we had.

The thought made me inexplicably sad, and I shrugged it off as a rough day. I never did like getting shot at.

When we got out, the driver informed me the rest of my team had set up at the beginning of the tree-lined lane leading to the house. No one would bother us while we were there. He helped me lug Leo past the fake flamingos in the yard and through the front door, all with Evelina complaining we were being too rough. He waited for his next instructions, and I told him he could go get something to eat if he wanted.

The most important thing was to get Leo patched up enough to get him back to the Everglades. He was in no shape to make the trip without some kind of medical intervention, especially since his feat of valor at the office building had stolen the last of his energy. I had to admit I was still impressed by his aim.

Speaking of being impressed, Evelina had wowed me with her quick action in both taking out the guy on the roof and alerting me to the other one so I wouldn't get shot. Even after seeing Leo in such a bad spot as dangling off a roof while unconscious, she'd kept it together.

And now she was busy gathering first aid supplies to help her brother. A trip to the hospital would have been ideal, but we couldn't risk it. Once he was stable enough to get him back to the island, I'd call in a favor from one of the doctors I knew.

"What can I do?" I asked when she had her tray full of supplies picked out.

She tossed me a bottle of rubbing alcohol, some gauze and cotton balls, and a tube of antiseptic cream. "Strip him down to his underwear so we don't miss anything. Don't worry, he'll only be pissed at me, and I can handle him. Start cleaning up the smaller cuts and wrap them in the gauze. If you think something needs stitches, just clean it and leave it, and I'll get to it. I'm going to start on his poor face."

I kept an eye on her as she worked, afraid seeing her twin in such a condition would be too much for her. But her hands were steady, and her gaze never wavered from what she was doing. Once she thought his face was cleaned up enough, she deftly threaded a needle with a long thread and ruthlessly plunged it through a gaping wound above his eyebrow.

"Can you just grab him if he wakes up," she said. "Nobody likes getting their face sewn up without anesthesia."

He was down for the count, though, so I went back to assess his other wounds. His shoulder might not have been broken after all, but a couple of ribs most certainly were. He had slash marks across his lower chest as if he'd been whipped, and I grew angrier as I kept finding new, gruesome injuries. I swabbed a couple of burns on his upper thighs and plastered gauze over them, then got to his calf, where I stopped and turned to Evelina in dismay.

"Shit," I said.

She didn't look up from her careful stitching. "What is it?"

"Those bastards shot him."

She swore. "I guess there's a first time for everything."

122

My mouth hung open. "Looks like the bullet's still in there," I repeated her curses. It was dangerous to leave it in there to possibly get infected. "I'm really sorry, but we can't risk taking him to the ER. It'll have to wait."

She shook her head, tying off the last tiny knot in his eyebrow. "I can get it out."

"You can? Since when?"

"Leo and I both took emergency first aid a couple years back. It comes in handy every now and then."

She moved down to stand beside me, nudging me out of the way. Pouring half the bottle of alcohol over the hole, she grabbed a pair of forceps from the tray and, without blinking, began to dig around in her brother's leg. I wasn't a squeamish man by any means, but the sight and sound of it made my stomach heave.

"Be prepared to hold him down," she said, leaning closer to get a better view. "People really don't like getting bullets taken out without anesthesia."

She chuckled humorlessly at her little joke, and I stayed ready to throw myself over Leo if he woke up. After what seemed like hours but was probably barely a minute, she straightened up with the small slug of lead brandished between the surgical pincers. As soon as she dropped it on the tray, she pressed a handful of gauze into the wound, now leaking blood.

"I'll just stitch this up now," she said, voice and eyes like ice, her hands steady as she threaded a fresh needle.

"Remind me to have you around if I'm ever nabbed by a rival and can't get to a hospital," I said, awestruck by her.

She didn't look up, only laughed again as she eased the needle through his flesh. There was a very real chance that I could love this woman.

Maybe I already did.

I kept cleaning the more superficial wounds and stayed on guard to hold Leo down if he woke up, all the while desperately trying to forget I just thought that. Love Evelina? Of course, I did. I always had. It was because of our history together that I'd always care for her, and yes, even love her like a—

123

No. It was more than that now, and I didn't think it was going to change back to the old fatherly affection any time soon. And it had to stop. Loving Evelina in the way I thought I did was more dangerous than any festering gunshot wound. Unequivocally, no matter what she might think about her doting father, I had no doubt that if Oleg ever found out about us, I'd be dodging his fists, at the very least, if not a bullet.

I had to find a way to end things without making her think she'd done anything wrong. Hell, maybe she'd be glad to be done with me since I still wasn't sure I wasn't just a fun way to pass the time while she was stuck in my care. I tried to pretend it was sympathy pain I was feeling as I kept watching her fix Leo up, but the pain was my own. I didn't want to lose her.

Once she'd gone over him from head to toe and deemed him as well as she could make him, she staggered back a few steps and put her face in her blood-covered hands. She wasn't as cold as ice. She was holding it all in until the job was done.

That impressed me most of all.

I guided her to the bathroom, all tacky pink and turquoise but with everything in working order, and held her hands under the cool water until all the blood had washed down the drain. I stood close enough to feel the deep trembling she was fighting to control. Our eyes met in the mirror, and hers filled with tears, but she fought to hold them back.

Turning off the water, I handed her a towel and gathered her in my arms. "You don't need to be strong anymore, Evelina," I said.

She collapsed against my chest, sobbing. I held her close and let my hand glide up and down her back, making small, soothing noises and just letting her ride out the storm. My heart felt full, holding her like that, but it also broke a little bit. I wanted to always be the one to be there for her in times like this, but I just couldn't.

She needed me right now, and I wouldn't let her down, but I had to end this soon before either of us got hurt beyond repair.

CHAPTER 21 - EVELINA

I sat on the cushy armchair beside Leo's bed and watched him sleep. The small room was a far cry from anything at the Everglades compound, with its palm frond wallpaper and thick turquoise wall-to-wall carpet. The old-fashioned pull-down shades were drawn, and the light of a single ceramic lamp on the bedside table lit the space. The multiple window air conditioning units worked overtime to keep the place cool. They created a soothing humming sound in the background.

Leo snored loudly through his broken nose, and I patted the sheet he was covered with just to have something to do. Despite it being an arguably awful day, I felt oddly content. I shouldn't have. My brother had been brutally beaten and almost fell to his death, Mikhail had been seconds from getting shot, and I had to kill someone. Even when someone deserved it, even when it meant saving my own life, I didn't like it.

I would have done it all over again, though, just like I knew Mikhail would. It was part of our lives. Over the hum of the air conditioners, I could hear him clattering around in the kitchen just down the hall, trying to fix us a meal. I had a feeling my sense of calm happiness mainly was to do with him.

I was overjoyed that Leo was safe now and going to be okay. Still, Mikhail's tender care during my breakdown after having to sew my brother back up gave me hope for a real future together. It was one thing when everything was fun and games in the bedroom, but he'd proven he was there for me through the worst of it as well.

What might that be like? A real future with Mikhail? I pushed aside the awkward thoughts that I knew plagued him. This was our life, after all, not Kristina's or my father's. Where would we live? As much as I loved the Everglades mansion, living there full-time would be inconvenient. I giggled softly at the thought of going through all those security checks just to run out for snacks.

I'd never seen where he lived full-time here in Miami, but the place he still owned in Moscow was beautiful. And I did have my investigative work there. Maybe we'd split our time between countries, and our children would, of course, be bilingual.

"What the hell are you daydreaming about?" Leo was awake and staring at me with a bemused expression on his busted face. Normally he was quite handsome, but now…

"You look like Frankenstein's monster," I said so I didn't have to admit what he'd caught me thinking about. "But I'm glad you're okay."

He was generous not to tell me it was no thanks to me that he was in that condition. "Where has Mikhail been hiding you?" he asked. "Not even Papa knew for sure."

I grinned, helping him sit up and pouring him a cup of water. "It's this huge compound out in the Everglades, like a cross between Yuri's mansion and a medieval castle, all surrounded by water and jungle." I described the ride on the airboat, the theater-sized TV screen, and the beautiful grotto with the luxurious pool. Instead of seeming excited, he looked suspicious. At least, I thought he did. It was hard to read him with all the swelling and stitches. Whatever he was thinking was making me nervous. "We're heading back there as soon as you're a little better. Did you know you got shot?"

He laughed, then held his aching face. "Yes, I know I got shot. Jesus. Do I have to go back to your swamp prison?"

"It's not a prison. It's really amazing, Leo. And Mikhail got my equipment back, so now that you'll be there, I think we can break that final layer of security I can't quite squeak through, and the three of us can take down the Novikoffs."

Now I was almost certain he looked suspicious. "Sure, I'm down with that since they tried to kill me and all, but since when has Mikhail been part of our team?"

I shrugged nonchalantly. "He's been a big help," I said.

"What's really going on? Don't forget I can read you like a book, Ev."

I feigned ignorance for about ten seconds, then couldn't hold out any longer. It had always been the hardest keeping my childhood crush a secret from Leo, but I hid it well and was almost certain he never had an inkling. When I spilled the beans, I was sure of it based on his shocked reaction.

"That's disgusting," he hissed, glancing at the door. "That son of bitch is lucky half my bones are broken, but he'd be wise not to let me have a gun again when he's around."

"Are you done?" I asked, struggling not to be hurt.

"No, actually," he continued. "Does Kristina know? She'd be furious. She'd kill you. God, Ev, gross. How much older is he?"

"Twenty years," I said quietly.

"Oh well, at least he's not Papa's age. Close, though."

"I don't care about the age difference. You know you're the only guy our age I've ever liked. He's a gentleman and mature and—"

"Stop," he interrupted. "I can't deal with this."

"You better learn to deal with it, or I'll put the bullet back in your leg and a new one in your gut." We stared each other down in silence, which I finally broke. "He makes me happy, Leo."

He made a retching noise, but I could tell he was teasing me now. "I knew you were acting way too giddy about being held against your will." He sighed and closed his eyes. "I'll try to keep an open mind, and I won't shoot him, but that's all I can promise for now."

"Okay," I said, leaning over to kiss the tiny spot on his forehead that didn't have a cut or bruise. "I'll take it."

"Go," he murmured. "I don't need you to hover around. You did a great job fixing me up, but I need to rest for now. I should be ready to go in the morning."

"We can stay longer if you're not up to it," I assured him.

He shook his head, eyes still closed. "The guys who grabbed me only wanted to know where you were, and I know they used me to get you out in the open."

"That's what Mikhail said."

"Well, he was right." Leo groped around for my hand. "Listen, they're not going to stop until you're dead, so the quicker you're back in the Everglades fortress, the better."

A few seconds later, his hand loosened, and he was once again fast asleep. I left to look for Mikhail in the cheery, orange-speckled Formica and oak-paneled kitchen. He was no longer in there, but a bowl of chicken salad was in the olive-green fridge. I put my hand on it but decided I was more tired than hungry and wanted to be with Mikhail.

I went down the hall to the second bedroom and pushed open the door, ready to fall into bed after the exhausting day. He sat in an armchair staring at the floor, his dark expression a sharp contrast to the bright floral bedspread next to him.

"Leo woke up," I said, hoping that would bring a smile. "He thinks he'll be ready to leave tomorrow. He says he just needs sleep."

"Good," he said, not looking up.

I chalked it up to the awful day and went to put my arms around him. Instead of drawing me closer, he stiffened. Something about his face wouldn't let me ask what was wrong.

Instead, I peeled off my top and stretched my arms over my head, about to pop out of my bra and waiting for him to notice. "Speaking of sleep," I said, feeling awkward all of a sudden. Normally when my top came off, his eyes came up, among other things. "Um, I can't wait to get in bed. Are you joining me?"

He finally looked up, his eyes darkening to see I was getting undressed, but instead of reaching for me, he shook his head. "We need to stop this, Evelina." His voice was rough, and he looked down again.

"What?" I asked, physically getting knocked back by his words. "Stop what?"

He shook his head. "Don't. You know."

I stared at him in confusion, which quickly turned to anger. "But I told my brother about us."

He groaned and ran his fingers through his hair. "I really wish you hadn't."

"Why are you doing this?" I asked, then held up my hand before he could answer, listing all his reasons in a voice dripping with sarcasm. "You're too old; I'm your daughter's best friend. You've known my father for too long."

"Yes, all of that," he said, ignoring my anger, which somehow worsened it. "You can dismiss it all you want, but those things are very real problems."

"Kristina wants you to be happy," I argued. "My father wants me to be happy." I paused, unsure he deserved to hear it, but I blurted it out anyway. "You make me happy, Mikhail."

He looked at me with eyes full of pain. As if he longed to drag me onto his lap and hold me tight. Or maybe that was what I wanted.

"It's not that simple. And that's not how fathers think, believe me."

"You're wrong," I said. "He'd come around."

"He'd kill me," he answered without missing a beat. "And I'd deserve it."

"I can't stand it," I said, only restraining myself from shouting because my brother was lying sick in the next room. I stamped my foot, and the plush carpet swallowed the sound. "I hate those old-fashioned notions."

He shrugged ruthlessly. "Well, they exist whether you hate them or love them. I hate them too, so there's that."

It was on the tip of my tongue to spit out that I hated him, but it would have been a lie. As angry as I was, I didn't hate him. "We're a great team," I said. "You know we are. You know you're going to regret this."

He jumped up and pinned me to the wall, his chest pressed hard against mine. "I already do, damn it."

Shocked at his sudden change, I took in a ragged breath, making his eyes drop to the lacy edge of my bra. Seeing the desire in his eyes that he kept fighting killed me. The feel of him pressed against me made me weak.

I slid my arms around his neck and stood on my toes so his mouth was closer. His hard length brushed against me as I rose, and he breathed out in a ragged huff. But he didn't move away.

"Please," I begged. "Just one more time."

Chapter 22 - Mikhail

What was this gorgeous, infuriating woman doing to me? I had spent what felt like hours in that darkened room, finally working up the resolve to end things with Evelina. I'd go back to being her protector, her best friend's father. Nothing more.

That resolve began to weaken the moment she came into the room. Tired from the long day, bedraggled from running around in a deserted building, and emotionally exhausted from the fear for her brother's life. And still, the most beautiful woman I'd ever seen. But our time had run its course. Hadn't it?

Why did I need to end things with her again? All the very real reasons made a lot more sense when she wasn't within touching distance. When I didn't have to look into her confused and hurt eyes. Then none of it made any sense.

She was right about us being a great team, damn it. I could so easily see a life with her. But it would have to be a life without my daughter, who'd surely cut me off. And it might not even be a very long life once Evelina's father found out. She thought I was exaggerating the force of his retribution, but I was probably downplaying it for her benefit.

She saw her doting father as a benevolent man who only wanted her happiness. And that was probably true as far as she was concerned. I, however, knew exactly how ruthless Oleg could be regarding *his* idea of what should make his daughter happy. I was not that thing. He would consider what I'd been doing with Evelina the worst breach of trust.

What if we chose to defy everyone else we loved? That probably sounded hopelessly romantic to someone Evelina's age, but we'd have to live on the run, cut off everyone we cared about. She'd resent me within a year, despise me after that, and we'd have ruined our family relationships for nothing.

I knew all of that. Been over it again and again. My brain fully accepted it, but my heart refused to comply. And the look in her eyes, the sound of her voice, and the way she clung to me made it impossible to resist.

One more time? Well, it better be a good one.

"Damn it, Evelina," I said, our lips inches apart. My cock throbbed against her, and she knew it, exploited my need for her.

"Please," she repeated.

I swore again. She tightened her arms around my neck, pulling herself closer. Our lips collided, her teeth nipping at my lower lip as my hands curled around the lacy cups of her bra. She pushed me backward, still on her toes, and I finally lifted her off her feet and swung her onto the bed. She laughed raucously, joyously, but I lightly clapped my hand over her mouth.

"Your brother," I reminded her. The fact she told him was bad enough. He might have pretended to take it in stride for her sake, but I highly doubted he needed to hear evidence of our affair.

"It's going to be hard to be quiet," she said, her breath hot and soft against my throat as I rolled her over me.

"Think of it as a challenge," I suggested, moaning when she wriggled her way down to my jeans.

"You try it first," she said, giving me a wicked look as she undid the button.

She kept eye contact while she slid down the zipper. Without glancing down, she freed my cock from my boxers and wrapped her palm around it. The first stroke made me jerk in her hand. The second made me groan. She teased me mercilessly, but I managed to stay reasonably quiet. She scowled, finally dropping her head to my chest.

"God, you're good," she said. "Maybe I'm not working hard enough."

She rose up to pop off her lacy bra and twirled her thumb and finger around her nipples, letting her head drop back. "Your turn, she said, wiggling out of her jeans and straddling me in a pale cotton thong. She pulled my hands up to replace hers.

"More than happy to have a turn," I said. As soon as I tweaked her taut nipples, she moaned and began grinding against me, her soft sounds getting higher pitched. And louder.

"Hush," I said, enjoying watching her but seriously not wanting her brother to hobble in and use the last of his strength to castrate me.

She licked her lips and looked down. "I think the only way I can keep quiet is if something's in my mouth."

I cracked up at her vixen act, but the laughter turned to a stifled yelp when she hopped off and switched positions, her lips wrapped around my cock, her ass in the air. I reached over and gave her ripe cheeks a light slap. She squealed around my shaft and arched her back even more. I smacked her a bit harder, throbbing at the sight of her pale little ass growing pink. Instead of spanking her again, I slid my hand between her thighs to find her clit through the damp cotton.

"Oh, God, yes," she murmured, licking around the tip of my cock as she moved her body against my fingertips. "What could feel better?"

"Is that a real question?" I asked.

The vibration of her soft laughter against my sensitive flesh made me nearly shoot down her throat. But if this was going to be our last time, there was no way it was ending so soon. I gripped both sides of her thong and snapped them off with a quick tug, then hoisted her so that hot little ass was right in my face. Pulling her backward, I licked a stripe up and down the length of her pussy, finding her opening and plunging my tongue in.

Her lips stilled around my cock as she gyrated her hips to give me better access to her slick heat.

"I can't concentrate," she gasped, pushing closer.

"Multi-task, baby," I teased, nibbling on her smooth cheek. "Or just let me keep licking you up and down."

Her breath came in quick, short pants, and she pressed her face into my thigh while I enjoyed her. The panting turned to soft mewling sounds that got louder and louder. As I pushed my tongue deeper, I gave her a little love tap on the side of her ass to remind her of the noise limits. She pressed her face against my thigh. A moment later, her teeth sunk into my leg. I could have stopped, but I was having too much fun. I tossed her a pillow, and she buried her face in it while I reached around to stroke her clit while I lapped at her with my tongue.

I laughed against her as a muffled scream came from the depths of the feather pillow. She went limp across my thighs, her legs spread on either side of my chest and arms akimbo, her face half obscured behind a flowery pillowcase. Truly a sight to behold. A sight I wanted to burn into my memory.

When would I ever have so much fun again?

She raised herself on shaking arms and turned around to straddle me again. Taking my face in her hands, she leaned over and kissed me. A deep, soul-stirring kiss.

"You're amazing," she whispered as she finally pulled away. We searched each other's eyes, recognizing the hint of sadness, but we both pushed it away. "Now fuck me harder than you ever have before," she said.

Or ever would again, I finished silently.

"Whatever you say," I told her, brushing her hair off her face and tucking the strands behind her ears. I leaned closer. "How have I never noticed how cute your ears are?"

I nibbled the soft lobe and kissed my way down her neck. I had definitely noticed before how much she liked that. I trailed my lips along her collarbone, running my thumbs back and forth over her breasts to bring her rosy nipples to tight peaks. Then I leaned back to just look at her.

"You're so beautiful," I said. "I don't have the words to tell you how damn beautiful you are."

She ran her fingers over my eyebrows and down my jaw. "Do you know how much I like your stubble?" she asked. "The way it looks and the way it feels."

I touched her cheek. "It makes your skin pink," I said. "Like how you blush when you ask what you want me to do to you."

"How many more silly things are we going to say to each other?" she asked, sliding back and forth over my cock.

"As many as we can think of."

Her head dropped to my shoulder. I was afraid she would cry, which would have killed me. Gripping her waist, I ran my palms up the sides of her body.

"These curves," I said appreciatively. "Like a goddess."

She nodded and looked back up. Her eyes were bright but free of tears. A slow smile curved her lips. "Everything," she said, voice thick with emotion I could feel down to my bones. "Everything about you."

Tangling my fingers in her hair, I tugged her head back. "I feel exactly the same, Evelina." I kissed her before she could answer. She reached down to take my cock in her hand, to guide it inside her. I shook my head and lifted her off me, placing her on her back. "I want to see your hair spilled out on the pillow," I told her.

With a smile, she shook her hair out and reached for me, pulling me down to her. "I can't wait anymore. Fuck me, Mikhail. You already know what I want."

I laughed; our bittersweet spell broken by her bossy tone. "Harder than I ever have before? Is that right?"

I didn't give her a chance to sass me back, spreading her legs and plunging my cock deep inside her. There were condoms in the bedside table drawer. The house was well equipped with anything someone might need. But I was reckless. Maybe I was hoping. It didn't matter. I just had to be inside her with nothing between us. This last time.

She held on, her arms tight around my shoulders and her face tucked against my neck while I gave her what she'd demanded. Hard and wild until she had to grab the pillow and clutch it against her face to muffle her screams of pleasure. Only then did I take my own, teeth clenched, head thrown back. I filled her until I was spent, kissing her wherever I could reach, going until nothing was left in me, and my muscles gave out.

I rolled to the side and pulled her close, not caring how sweaty we were. Tucking the sound barrier pillow under her head, I watched her until her eyes slowly closed. A few moments later, she was breathing evenly, fast asleep. As tired as I was, I kept my eyes trained on her, taking in the gentle sound of her breaths.

Ignoring the looming regrets racing toward me at the speed of a deadly avalanche, I just watched, listened, and savored this last time I'd ever get to hold her like this.

CHAPTER 23 - EVELINA

I woke up from pleasant dreams, my body tingling from even better memories. Until I thought a little further back and remembered that Mikhail wanted to end things. As much as I tried to pretend he'd come around, he had seemed deadly serious about last night being the last time for us to be together. I had no choice but to believe him. Emptiness threatened to overwhelm me. All I could do was push aside all my feelings and hurry up and get dressed.

As soon as I was out of the shower and in some fresh clothes from the safe house closet, Leo hobbled into the bedroom doorway on crutches that were too short for him. He looked worse than the day before, but that was normal, with bruises and contusions. I tried to hide a grimace, glad to see him up and about. I hated seeing him brought low, even more so when it was my fault.

"Hurry up," he said. "Everything hurts, and Mikhail promised he'd get a real doctor to check me out and give me some meds once we're back at the fortress."

I hoped he wouldn't be disappointed after my glowing review of the place.

"Were you waiting for me? Why didn't you wake me up?" A glance at the clock showed it was almost ten, not exactly the crack of dawn.

"Mikhail wouldn't let me. There are some eggs left if you're hungry." He waved one of his crutches toward the kitchen.

I didn't know how I felt about that tiny bit of consideration. It was probably nothing, and better to keep any feelings at bay for now.

Overanalyzing would get me nowhere. "I'll just pour some dry cereal in a bag since you're in such a hurry."

"Good," he said.

"Ingrate," I muttered.

"Sorry, what?" he asked, pretending like he hadn't heard me.

I kept my lips zipped. Yes, I had patched him up, but I was still the reason he needed patching. Mikhail wasn't in the kitchen or the sunken living room, either. When Leo noticed me looking around, he told me he'd headed out to coordinate with the security team. I tried to act normal and not like the rug had just been torn out from under me, and my heart felt as bruised as Leo's face. I couldn't believe I was glad he found Mikhail and me being together so distasteful that he didn't ask me any questions.

Shortly after I forced myself to eat a reheated omelet, Mikhail returned and hustled us out to the car as if he hadn't been the one to let me sleep in that morning. Leo stretched out in the third row, and I sat ahead of him with a cooler full of cold water and snacks. Another small consideration? Or Mikhail just didn't want to have to stop?

At the last second, he climbed in the front next to the driver. After Leo fell asleep almost as soon as we were on the highway, Mikhail turned around and faced forward the rest of the mostly silent drive back to the compound. I didn't bother trying to engage him in conversation because what was there to say? He was done with me, and I had to deal with it.

Back at the mansion, as soon as I made sure Leo was settled in a room just a few doors down from mine, I made a beeline for my computer. The sweet lull of going over all the surveillance footage that was recorded while we were gone was just what I needed. I could always count on work to improve things at least slightly.

I only looked up from my screen when the doctor arrived, and right after I showed him where Leo was, I hurried back down again. I might have wondered where Mikhail was, but I forced myself not to. The next time I looked up, the sun was in a different spot in the sky, and three hours had passed when I checked the time on the screen.

I rubbed my scratchy, dry eyes and went to stand by the window. Looking at all the green foliage and blue sky helped with the strain of staring at blurry video footage for hours on end. A corner of the swimming pool was visible from my office window, and I thought I might see Mikhail down there. Not that I missed him desperately already.

God, I needed help. It was better not to see him. The longer I went without contact, the more my cravings would lessen. It was like a sugar detox. Just had to go cold turkey. I heard a familiar thumping and turned to see my brother swinging in on new crutches that fit him better. He had a sling around one arm, but it hung loose so he could use the crutches. He wore baggy nylon basketball shorts and a garish Hawaiian shirt unbuttoned enough to reveal tightly wrapped ribs. His face was still a raw hamburger mess, but he looked relaxed and happy.

"Painkillers?" I asked.

He nodded. "That and antibiotics. He said your stitches were pretty good but wondered if you sterilized the needle."

"Of course, I did! Where did you get those clothes?" They certainly weren't Mikhail's. And Leo wasn't a slouch in the style department, either.

"The doc brought them. I think they might have been from the hospital lost and found."

"Well, as long as you're comfortable."

"Flying high, but not so much I can't take a look at what you've got." He made his way to my desk, and I pulled up another chair for him.

He immediately pulled up his code, frowning at the patches I'd made as he found them and jotting down notes on one of my sticky pads. "Remind me not to let you ever babysit my kids if I have any," he said, muttering about my subpar coding skills.

"You abandoned me," I said. "I did what I had to do to keep the cameras online."

He flinched, then turned to me. "I'm sorry about that. I should have stayed with you, not be a little bitch and cut you off like that."

My throat closed up at his unexpected remorse, and I shook my head. "No, I'm sorry." I waved my hand at his many injuries. "This is all my fault."

"Don't," he said. "This is those bastard Novikoffs' fault, no one else's. So, let's get to work to finish them."

I turned one of my monitors to face him and let him have the keyboard so he could fix whatever he thought was broken in his software code, and I kept running through the footage. We sat in companionable silence, and it felt like we were at home for a while, and my heart hadn't been broken.

"Need any more help?"

I looked up at the sound of Mikhail's voice to see him standing in the doorway. He'd been helping me quite a bit by sorting data into categories. Even though it felt like a knife was twisting in my chest at the sight of him, I nodded.

Leo gave me an odd look as if wondering what happened to my voice. "Come on in," he called.

Mikhail kept looking at me, waiting for explicit permission to get any closer. Or maybe it hurt him just as much to be near me. Then why come and ask if he could help? I should have told him we had it covered, but I waved him in.

"You can just do what you've been doing," I said stiffly. It was like my mouth didn't work properly. "Take my spot at the desk."

I got up to move to the couch, but he hurried to stop me. "No, it's fine. You need to watch the footage. I can do my thing on this side of the desk like usual."

He pulled up a chair and dragged the stack of files over. I stared at him until the pain in my chest reached a point I had to take a deep breath. All the while, he studiously avoided looking at me. This was a bad idea. It was worse than us hating each other. This felt almost dishonest. And Leo could sense the weird tension, giving me odd looks, probably wondering why Mikhail and I were being so stiff and polite to each other.

I scowled at Leo, and he shrugged it off. "The sooner we find out what we need to bring these scumbags down, the sooner we can get back to normal," he said.

"Agreed," Mikhail piped up, smiling at Leo and then starting to sort the files.

Okay, then. It seemed like the thing I wanted more than anything else was well and truly over. However, I still had my mission to take over the Novikoff territory. That had been the most important thing to me not so long ago, even though it felt like a lifetime had passed. I got back to work, hating the awkward atmosphere that crackled between Mikhail and me across the desk, but I wouldn't have changed it. It was better than nothing at all.

Chapter 24 - Mikhail

After a few days, nothing was better. It still caused a deep ache in my chest whenever I crossed paths with Evelina. Every morning I woke up determined to stay away. It wasn't like I didn't have plenty to do. The planned vacation time I set aside was long over, and I was getting calls from both my people in Miami and in Moscow with questions about what to do about this or that. If I didn't start showing my face around town soon, my enemies might grow bold again.

I could have stayed away from her, even moved to the other side of the house. But I knew that from the beginning, and it didn't work then, either. Every morning I had the best intentions to guard my heart, but by evening I was seeking her out. I used to think she was torturing me, but now I was the one looking for the pain.

It was better than nothing, and now that her brother was back, they both swore they were on the verge of a significant breakthrough in the Novikoff project. If that was true, it meant she'd be out of danger soon. I should have wanted that. Why did I want to keep her locked away with me when it only caused both of us so much anguish?

I saw the pain in her eyes, the downturn of her mouth. The fact she only wore baggy sweatpants and oversized shirts was only partly because of her brother's arrival. Every time I caught her looking at me, wistful and full of longing, it nearly broke me not to reach for her. Start pretending once again that there was a chance for us.

Having Leo around as a buffer while we worked on her surveillance operation would have been a relief, but her twin's curious and sometimes resentful looks bothered me. It was awkward that she'd told him, to say the least, but now that things were clearly over, it was worse. He was fiercely protective of her, just as she was of him, and being a guest in the man's home who broke your sister's heart must have rankled him.

I wouldn't fight him if it came to that, and if the kid wanted to take a swing at me once he was back to full capacity, I was resigned to letting him. And I really shouldn't have thought of him as a kid since he and Evelina were the same age. But she was so much more mature I truly often forgot the twenty years between us. She was an old soul despite her often-impetuous actions. An old soul I hoped I hadn't gravely injured with my own immature inability to control myself around her.

Maybe I imagined all her hurt looks. Maybe I was assuaging my own ego because my pain was so great. Maybe she was already well over me.

My phone rang, and I blinked, realizing I was still sitting out in the garden with my latest whiskey on the rocks. The ice had long since melted, and the glass was drenched in condensation. I frowned at the lowering sun beyond the acres of palms and cypresses. The time on my phone told me it was nearly dinner time. I'd been sitting out there stewing in my misery for hours. Whiling away the time until I couldn't stand it anymore and went to look for Evelina.

The call was from Kristina. She was currently in Honolulu, where I'd booked her into a resort under the guise of an early birthday present. She went along with it, not wanting to ask if something was still wrong any more than I wanted to answer. The one condition for her surprise vacation was that she checked in with me once a day.

"Hey Papa," she said cheerily, the sound of the surf crashing in the distance. "I just threw my towel down on the sand to bake all day."

"Don't forget sunscreen," I said.

"You sound just like my agent," she laughed. Oh good, this again. "Seriously, you'd really like her. She's just divorced and won't be single for long."

I smiled at my daughter's new obsession with matchmaking. Did she sense the recent sadness I had been trying to keep from her? She was always an intuitive person. The thought of meeting someone when my heart was so raw, let alone a talent agent, was completely untenable. I'd only compare the poor woman to Evelina; she'd only come up short.

"We'll see, sweetie," I said, realizing I was pulling one of those soft lies I'd admonished Evelina for. "But probably not," I added.

"I hate thinking about you being alone. And don't say you're always surrounded by people. Bodyguards don't count."

"You don't ever have to worry about me," I told her. I didn't need this new layer of heartache.

"I know. I consider it a hobby."

I laughed, the first genuine one in days. "Take a surfing lesson instead," I said. "But be careful. And don't—"

"Forget sunscreen. Bye, Papa."

The smile my daughter brought to my face faded as soon as she ended the call. What if she was trying to fix me up with her agent because she considered the woman to be like a mother figure? Did she need that in her life, even at her age?

I had almost pulled out half my hair over the last few days, and now I sunk my head into my hands. Yet another reason why I couldn't have Evelina. As if I needed more.

It was dinner time, and I was hungry, ignoring the last few meals. I should have gone to the kitchen and made a plate to take back out here or up to my room. Anywhere but the dining room where Evelina and her brother would be. If I could go a little bit longer without seeing her, I might be able to resist going to her office later, where I'd sneak pathetic glances at her while I did the busywork she gave me just to keep me in the room. It was gut-wrenchingly pathetic.

"Damn it," I snarled, getting up and storming to the dining room.

As if I would have been able to resist.

The twins were already sitting across from one another at the dining table, as different as they were alike. Leo looked fresh from the pool, his hair damp and combed back off his head. I had heard his sister admonishing him several times already for taking his rib bandages off to go in the water and crabbing at him that it probably wasn't suitable for his stitches, either. And as usual, he did exactly what he wanted anyway. They definitely had stubbornness in common.

Surprisingly, Evelina had ditched the oversized tees and was wearing a halter top tied in a bow behind her neck. It was one of my favorite looks on her, showing off her shapely shoulders and giving me the bonus of imagining untying the bow and watching the fabric slip down...

That had to stop.

"Oh, good, you're joining us," Leo said.

I gave him the benefit of the doubt and assumed he wasn't being sarcastic. Sometimes we really seemed to hit it off. For instance, we were both big hockey fans. We spent a good few hours the other evening in a friendly argument over who were the best players in the Russian leagues. At least, I thought it was friendly.

I had the choice to sit on Leo's side, Evelina's side, or at the head of the table. It shouldn't have been so difficult, but I paused in the doorway, wondering if I should just bid them a good evening and finish off my bottle of whiskey so I could pass out early.

"Come and sit down," Evelina said invitingly, patting the chair beside her while she gave Leo a scathing look.

Because she asked me to, I did. A moment later, the cook came in with a delicious-smelling dish and flung the cover off the tray with a flourish.

"Fantastic," Leo exclaimed. "You really outdid yourself, Olga. Thank you."

She beamed at him and started ladling the solyanka into his bowl. "I hope you like it, and it reminds you of home, Leo," she said.

So, he was not only on a first-name basis with my Swedish cook, but he'd also charmed her into learning a traditional Russian dish.

"I'm sure it's going to be perfect," he answered, making her smile grow even wider.

Evelina and I exchanged a look, both of us rolling our eyes simultaneously, then smothering a laugh. Just as quickly, she stopped and stared at her water glass as if it held all of life's secrets.

I got a call as we finished the savory soup, thick with fresh vegetables and meats. "Sorry," I said. "It's the head of security out at the wall."

Evelina and I exchanged another quick glance, this time one of anxiety. I answered the call, listening to what he had to say. "Someone's at the gate?" I repeated, for Evelina and Leo's benefit, in case they had to spring into action. "I didn't invite anyone, and I'm not expecting anyone," I told him. I was about to tell my guard to escort him back over the bridges and give him a good scare never to return, but Leo set his spoon down with a clatter.

"It's Papa," he said.

"Shit," Evelina and I both uttered at the same time. I told the guard to hang on, setting the phone aside and staring at her brother for an answer.

"What in the hell, Leo?" Evelina asked so I didn't have to.

"I was video chatting with him, and he just happened to notice I look like I went through a meat grinder, so I had to admit what happened."

"You didn't have to video chat with him," Evelina hissed.

"Yes, I did, because he thought it was weird that I refused, then he got worried, and I didn't want that, so I hopped on video so he'd know I was okay."

"But you're not okay, idiot," she said.

"What's with you two and treating your father like he's on his deathbed? He's not that old, for Christ's sake."

Leo gave us each a pointed look. "What's the big deal that he's here?" he asked, turning to his sister. "Huh, Evelina?"

She remained silent, and I was forced to admit it wasn't a big deal. I got back on the phone and told the guard to send me a picture of him. A second later, a photo of Oleg looking irritated popped up on my phone. "Let him through," I said, my stomach sinking.

"Oh God," Evelina groaned softly.

My sentiments exactly. Only Leo kept eating his dessert as if nothing was wrong because his conscience was clean. I only hoped I didn't exude guilt from every pore when I interacted with my old friend for the first time after sleeping with his daughter.

She seemed to sense what I was thinking and got up, tossing her napkin onto the table with more force than necessary. "I'll be in my office," she said, storming out.

Leo gave me an arch look around a big bite of apple cake. All I could do was shake my head at him. And get ready for the beating of a lifetime.

***

Oleg Morozov arrived with his own bodyguard and enough luggage to signal a long visit. After he hugged Leo and was informed that Evelina was working, he greeted me with a warm clap on the back.

"I can't thank you enough for snatching this boy of mine from the jaws of death and keeping Evelina safe all this time. She must have been a real handful."

Leo snorted, and I suppressed a sigh. "It's no problem, Oleg. I think of them as my own."

Another snort from Leo made my stomach drop. There was no way he didn't spill everything to his father. It was probably the real reason he got him here. I waited for my punishment for toying with Evelina's heart, but Leo only said he'd show Oleg to his room.

"Ah yes, I need a short rest after that long flight and all that driving. We'll catch up later over the good vodka I brought from home, eh, Mikhail?"

"Absolutely," I said.

All I could do was act like everything was normal until it wasn't. With nothing left to do but wait for the consequences of my actions, I went to help Evelina as I had been every evening.

I paused in the doorway of her office, finding her standing up and leaning over her desk, her fingers flying over the keyboard. I had seen her do this a couple times before. When she was just about to crack into a new camera system or solve a complex problem, her chair couldn't contain her.

She didn't seem to notice me, so I watched her work for a moment. I was enamored by every facet of her, especially this drive she had. If things were different, I'd massage her shoulders. They always got so tense when she was that deep in concentration. But things were how they were, and I stayed put.

She finally squealed and looked up, her shining eyes focusing on me. Hurrying around the desk, she grabbed my hand and pulled me to the computer. "I'm in," she said, dancing in place. "I finally cracked the final layer. Everything the Novikoffs own is mine. Total access, Mikhail."

Seeing her delighted made me happy, though I selfishly wished I was making her smile like that.

"I knew you'd get there," I said.

She flung her arms around me, vibrating with infectious excitement. I swung her around in a circle just to celebrate. This was what we'd been working for since I got her computers back for her. Well, she had been working for it. I was no better than a trained monkey sorting through piles of paper, but I felt a small part of her pride.

The feel of her against me had me reeling, and I couldn't let go. She didn't let go either, even when I set her feet back on the floor. I closed my eyes, savoring the sensation of her body sliding down mine. She still didn't let go, and I looked down to see her gazing up at me with parted lips.

"You're amazing," I said. "Brilliant and talented and gorgeous."

The next thing I knew, we were locked in an embrace, tongues tangling. Her leg slid up to wrap around my hip, and I gripped her behind to bring her even closer.

"What in the name of all that's holy is this?"

The furious shout made us jump apart. Evelina sucked in a breath, and I turned to face my best friend, who looked like he was about to pounce and tear me apart.

"What have I just seen?" he demanded; face so red it was closer to purple.

"Calm down," Evelina said, holding out her hands.

"Be quiet," he snapped, his glare centered only on me. I opened my mouth and shut it again. What was there to say?

He threw himself forward, covering the short distance with his hands outstretched like he wanted to throttle me. We'd gone after mutual enemies together, and I'd still never seen him so full of rage.

"Papa, stop," Evelina shouted, jumping in between us. I swiftly pushed her out of the way so she didn't suffer collateral damage that would only make Oleg angrier. "Papa, don't do this. It's not what you think. I love him!"

My head swiveled around, taking my eyes off the stalking beast. What did she just say? It didn't matter because Oleg's fist smashed into my face.

CHAPTER 25 - EVELINA

I was shocked to see my father launch at Mikhail, even more, shocked that he just wouldn't stop hitting him no matter how much I shouted or dragged at his shoulders. He only pushed me away, his fury like nothing I'd ever seen before. I had always thought of my father as an old man, and it was probably true that Leo and I coddled him a bit.

He wasn't a frail old man at all; he was solid. The force of each blow had me wincing. Seeing him this ruthless, a way I knew he must be in order to maintain his position in the Bratva but that he'd always taken care to shield us from, I realized he wasn't so much older than the man I wanted to spend the rest of my life with. Grayer, with a bit of a paunch, but still perfectly capable of causing real harm if Mikhail didn't start defending himself.

"Papa, please stop."

The blows only seemed to rain down faster. I finally ran to the hall and yelled for Leo.

God, men were stupid.

I couldn't stand it anymore. By the time Leo descended the stairs on his crutches, Mikhail might have been in a coma. I jumped on my father's back and held on as tightly as possible, hoping to choke some sense into him. He jerked back, and I flew off, hitting the floor with a hard thud. I coughed and rolled over to see both of them at my side, hovering to see if I was okay. Well, at least that got my father to stop—

Nope. As soon as he saw I was fine, he jumped on Mikhail again, shouting about betrayal.

Enough was enough. I hurried to the desk drawer and took out the gun I kept after we rescued Leo. Jerking open the sliding glass door, I stepped onto the balcony and fired a round into the air.

Turning back to look inside, I saw my father frozen with his fist in mid-air. Within seconds, the room was swarmed with guards.

"Oh, now you come running," I said bitterly.

Keeping a firm grip on the gun, I told them everything was fine. I gave my father a filthy glare until he nodded. Mikhail grunted for them to go, spitting blood onto the floor. Now it was just the three of us again, and no one was getting pummeled, but I kept the gun in my hand as I stepped back into the room.

"Evelina put the gun down," Mikhail said, sitting up with some effort.

"Shut up," my father and I said in unison.

He shrugged and hauled himself to sit on the couch, blood seeping from his nose. It took everything I had not to rush to his side and start sopping up the mess, but I had a bigger mess to take care of first. I turned to my father.

"No one took advantage of me. No one was betrayed." When he opened his mouth, I twitched my gun hand, and he closed it again. "I'm a grown woman, and you have to see that eventually. I'll pick who I want to be with. And I shouldn't have to be holding a gun for you to listen to me say it, either."

He was silent for a long time, looking at me mournfully and at Mikhail with murderous rage. "Over my dead body," he finally said, stalking from the room.

My heart seemed to turn to stone. Mikhail looked at me and sighed. He didn't say he told me so, but he may as well have since he got up and also left. I stood there all alone with the gun still in my hand. I put it back in the drawer and looked at my computer screen, barely remembering the joy I felt a few minutes ago when I finally succeeded at my goal.

Leo stumped in and over to my side. "I saw the last part. It went about as well as could be expected."

"Oh, fuck off," I said, then started to cry. There was no use trying to hide it; Leo could tell how miserable I was.

"Aw, Ev, I'm sorry," he said, pulling me into a rough, brotherly hug.

I was glad someone was left to offer comfort, but I wished I could go a few days without needing any.

CHAPTER 26 - MIKHAIL

I stormed past Leo on my way out of Evelina's office, and he gave me a death glare before going into it. A moment later, I heard her start to cry, and I stopped in my tracks, feeling like my skin was being ripped off. It was far worse than the multiple punches I just took, and my face hurt plenty. Things went exactly as I expected. Well, I was still alive, but that was probably only because Evelina had drawn a gun.

I was alive for now, anyway.

I trudged upstairs to clean up my face as best as I could. The damage wasn't too bad, but I'd rival Leo in the looks department for the next few days. It was almost as if Oleg was pulling his punches, but why? Trying to keep me alive until he figured out how he really wanted to end me, no doubt.

I was torn in two. Was any of it worth it? Friendship destroyed; love lost.

Did Evelina really blurt out that she loved me?

I was certain she was just passing the time or playing out a fantasy while I was the one getting caught up in feelings. Was she telling the truth or trying to defuse the situation?

After giving Oleg some time to cool off, I sought him out and tried to make things right. Or at least less wrong. Or let him get the murder over with. I wasn't one to cower in my own house, no matter what might be waiting for me when I found him.

He was sitting in one of my favorite spots in the garden, the bottle of vodka he'd brought from Moscow on the arm of the chair, a currently empty shot glass on the table in front of him. Based on the level of the liquid in the bottle, he'd already had a few, but he was a man who could hold his alcohol, just like I was.

I cleared my throat as I stepped into the seating area, so he wouldn't think I was sneaking up on him. He turned and scowled at me but made no new move to attack, so I sat in a chair just out of arm's reach.

"You did promise me some of that," I said, pointing to the bottle.

Oleg grumbled but reached beside him, pulled out another shot glass, begrudgingly filled it, and then handed it to me.

"I see you brought two glasses with you," I said.

My old friend, possibly my new enemy, shrugged. "Leo told me you made Evelina cry."

"I'm pretty sure it was you who did that," I retorted.

His eyes narrowed at me, and he refilled his glass, drained it, then shook his head. So, no answer to that?

I swallowed the fine Russian vodka and broke the silence. "I admire and respect Evelina. She's a grown woman now, who wants to make her own choices," I said since I couldn't exactly tell him she'd practically thrown herself at me.

He took a deep breath and clenched his fists but didn't swing at me again. He was still glaring, though. "She thinks she loves you, and now her heart will be broken."

"Does it have to be?" I asked, not sure I dared to hope but in a bad enough place to press my luck.

Oleg reached for my glass and refilled it. "Ah, but you said you only admire and respect her."

"God damn it, Oleg." I knocked back the vodka and returned his glare with one of my own. "Of course, I love her. It's probably insane, but there it is. I've never felt this way. Surely, I don't have to list all her good qualities—"

"No, you don't." He slammed his hand on the arm of the chair. "Of course, I know how amazing my daughter is."

"What happens if I choose a life with Evelina?" I asked, throwing all my cards on the table, so to speak. "If she chooses a life with me," I added.

150

There was an interminable pause while he stared out at the palms. "You risk death if you hurt her," he said. "But I'd say that to anyone, even someone I deemed more suitable for her."

"She seems to think I'm plenty suitable for her." If he didn't kill me for that, I'd probably live through the night, at least.

He only sighed and kept staring straight ahead. I had nothing more to say for the moment, and the only sounds were the swish of the breeze in the palm fronds and the never-ending chorus of frogs and cicadas out in the swamp. Then his phone pinged. And pinged again, repeatedly.

He picked it up and read the messages, chuckling. "I've just had a lot of money mysteriously show up in several of my accounts. Looks like Evelina's gotten into Novikoff's bank. He'll be dry by morning and never know what hit him." He looked up and laughed ruefully. "That's how the kids destroy each other these days. Not with guns but a bunch of gibberish on a screen that I'll never understand."

"You're not that old, Oleg." I was proud of Evelina and wished I could congratulate her properly.

"You just say that because you're a lot closer to my age than Evelina's," he said.

"Ouch," I answered.

"Hurt as bad as your face?"

"Almost," I admitted.

We lapsed into a companionable silence, sipping the vodka and listening to the sounds of the Everglades. After a few more glasses, Oleg got up to go to sleep, remaining silent as he left the garden. We were at an impasse. No blessing, but no more threats, either.

I sat alone a good while longer, not wanting to face an empty bed when I'd grown used to having Evelina in it.

CHAPTER 27 - EVELINA

Leo and I watched the last of the Novikoff's offshore accounts transfer to our father's anonymous Cayman Islands account, where I'd disperse it so the Russian government wouldn't look too closely at the insane amount of money pouring in.

We'd been wreaking havoc most of the night, and it helped keep my mind off my father acting like a caveman or Mikhail just walking away like he did.

After we cracked into several members of the upper echelon's phones, we faked dozens of conflicting messages, sowing distrust, sending them scurrying all over New York and generally causing mayhem within their organization. The final nail in their coffin was anonymously sending a massive packet of information to the NYC police that would shut down at least a few of their businesses.

"By morning, they'll be broke," Leo said, offering me a fist to bump.

"And won't know up from down," I agreed. "Ripe for the picking."

"What do you want to do next?" He struggled to stay awake, pretending he wasn't tired so I wouldn't have to be alone. But I had noticed him beginning to wilt at least an hour ago.

"Let's call it a night," I said.

His brow furrowed. "You sure you'll be all right?"

"Yes, I'm fine. Go to bed. But promise you'll back me up when we talk to Papa about me being the one to swoop in and pick up the pieces of our devastated rival, okay?"

"Pick over the bones, you mean. But of course. You earned it, Ev. You're going to do great up there."

I forced a big smile because he expected me to be delighted about our complete and utter victory. And I should have been. This had been the most important thing to me, and now it seemed rather empty. It was all I had since Mikhail wasn't going to fight for me. I'd prove to my father I could be a good leader and find satisfaction that way.

"Oh, Leo," I called before he got out the door. He turned, ready to do anything for me. It was nice having a twin brother, someone who'd never let me down. "Let me use your phone, will you?"

"Sure," he said, tossing it to me. "But don't read my sexts with Natalia Obolensky. Trust me."

"Gross," I said, horrified. "Why would you even tell me you were doing such a thing?"

"Because I know you get curious, but believe me, you don't want to know what disgusting things we say to each other."

I picked up a pen and threw it at him. "Ugh, get out."

He ducked the projectile and thumped his way out on his crutches, laughing. I scrolled through his contacts until I found Kristina, and my resolve wavered as my thumb hovered over the call button. I had to do this. We'd never kept secrets from each other, and I wouldn't jeopardize our friendship for the world. She was as important to me as Leo was.

"Oh God," I groaned, close to chickening out. Why was I doing this? Mikhail wouldn't tell her if his life depended on it. My father certainly didn't spend time gossiping with her, and Leo was loyal to the marrow.

My heart hurt, and I needed my best friend. Even if she hated me, I had to try to make her understand. And maybe, hopefully, she wouldn't hate me. I pressed the button.

"Leo?" she answered tentatively. "What's wrong? Is everyone okay?"

"It's me," I said. "I... lost my phone, so I had to use Leo's."

"Evelina!" she shrieked. "I was starting to get worried. I knew you were on a job, but you never go quiet this long."

She kept talking in a rush—It seemed like she was in Hawaii. It was so good to hear her voice. "Hey, Kristina," I finally interrupted. "I have to tell you something."

She knew instantly that it was serious and told me to go ahead. She said she suspected something was wrong because why else would her father pay for an acting workshop and then send her to a swanky resort in Honolulu.

"It was me," I admitted. "I had a price on my head. But they're taken care of now, so you'll probably be able to go home soon. And about your dad...."

She chattered about wanting to set him up with her agent, and my stomach was tied in knots. Of course, my having a hit put out on me didn't faze her now that the threat was over. It was par for the course in our lives.

"Stop," I broke in. "I can't listen to you talk about setting your dad up with some accomplished talent agent."

"Why not?"

This was it. I swallowed hard. "Because I'm in love with him."

I held the phone away while she howled with laughter. When she realized I wasn't joining in, she said, "What the fuck? Are you serious? Umm, that's disgusting. I mean, I knew you had that little crush on him in eighth grade, but come on, that was ten years ago."

How did she know when I'd guarded it so carefully? I bought him that stupid, expensive bottle of cologne for Christmas. Of course. "Please don't hate me," I begged. "My dad had him bring me to his Everglades place until the heat was off, and... some stuff happened."

She was silent for so long that I checked to see if the call was dropped. Then she roared with anger. "Do not tell me that. This is a cruel joke, Ev. It has to be. It's sick. He's like your dad. He *is* my dad. What now? Are you going to be my stepmom?"

She really sounded like she might throw up. Why was this so difficult for the people closest to me to accept? Was I such a monster for loving a wonderful man?

"No," I said, voice cracking. "It's over. He dumped me."

"Do not say my *father* dumped you like you're both in high school. You had a fling, and now it's over, and you had no reason to—damn it, are you crying?"

I was. I was sobbing. Sitting on the floor and bawling my eyes out. It was bad enough I had to get over Mikhail. But another stupid decision had cost me one of the most important people in my life.

"I'm sorry," I choked. "I'm sorry I told you. But I needed a friend because everything hurts."

Silence again. "I'm still your friend," she said. A bit tersely, but she said it.

"Thank you."

"I'm not going to lose it again. Just start from the beginning and tell me everything, and don't take it personally if you hear me gag."

I laughed and rubbed away my tears. I hadn't lost Kristina after all. I started from the beginning, yes, all the way back to when we first met. I had to find a charger and sit by the outlet as I kept telling her everything, all my feelings for Mikhail, all the reasons I thought we were right for each other. Everything up to the point my dad started bashing his face in.

"Holy crap, your dad knows?"

"Yes. It sucks. Everything sucks."

"And my dad just walked away?" She sounded indignant on my behalf, and I had to admit it felt good. "Do I need to talk to him?"

"Oh God, no. Please don't. It's just nice to talk to you about it, that's all."

We finally moved on to other subjects, and after two hours, my throat was raw from all the talking. I promised to call her again as soon as I was back in New York, which would hopefully be soon.

I was so happy Kristina didn't hate me, and I wouldn't have to hide such an important part of my life from her. It was short-lived, but I'd never forget my time with Mikhail.

It was late, but I was so amped up from my total domination of the Novikoffs and coming clean to Kristina that I knew I'd never get to sleep. I was still too pissed off at my dad to go talk to him, and positive Mikhail would turn me away if I sought him out.

What was left? I sat at my desk and amused myself, watching the surveillance cameras I still had control over. The Novikoffs were going nuts trying and failing to get a handle on things, which was a small ray of sunshine.

When I looked up a short while later, I was surprised to see Mikhail standing in the doorway, watching me with a look I couldn't decipher. His bruises looked awful, but he was still the most handsome man I'd ever seen. They gave him a rugged, bad-boy air. God, I was pathetic.

"Are you drunk?" I asked.

"Why would you say that?"

I nodded to the bottle in his hand. "Half empty bottle of vodka, that's why."

"This is not all my doing," he said, entering the office and putting the bottle on my desk. "And yes, I'm slightly drunk. But I've never been so clear." He held up his phone. "I'm wondering if you can tell me why I got a cryptic text from my daughter telling me she just wants me to be happy?"

I looked away, worried he was going to get mad at me. Then I shrugged. So what if he was mad? He had no claim on who I talked to or what I said. "I told Kristina," I admitted.

He didn't look angry, just perplexed. "Why do that? Why upend everything for a fling?"

Oh, talk about angry. The fury hit me harder than the punches he took to the face earlier. I didn't owe him an answer and was too mad to be able to formulate one. I stormed past him before I added to his collection of bruises.

At the door, he caught up to me and grabbed my hand, reaching past me to shut the door. I jerked my hand out of his, and he pushed me against the door, caging me in with a hand on each side of my shoulder. "Why turn everything inside out for a fling?" he repeated.

More than anything, I wished I hated him so I could slap or kick him, but all I wanted was for him to kiss me. I knew I could make him, but I was sick to death of the heartache I'd have tomorrow when he refused to see how great we were together and acted full of regret.

I tipped my chin up defiantly. "You tell me why you think I did it."

His brows nearly met over his dark eyes. "Do you love me, Evelina?"

"Answer that question yourself," I demanded. "Because you know me. Just like I know you."

Our lips were inches apart, our bodies so close together a breath would have brought his chest to mine.

"You love me," he said. Not a question, but his voice was full of wonder.

I nodded. "And?"

His lip curled slightly. "And I love you."

My heart kicked into high gear. He'd finally said the words I had longed to hear most of my life but never dared to dream about, even in my wildest fantasies. He slid his hands down my shoulders and gripped my hips, dragging me close to him.

"I love you," he repeated. "Now say it back."

I pushed away enough so that I could look into his eyes. He stared at me, unblinking, maybe not breathing. "I love you," I said.

His mouth crashed down onto mine. I grabbed his shoulders and all but climbed his body, wrapping my arms around his neck. His tongue nudged my lips, and I opened to him, sighing as he dragged me backward.

"Where?" he asked raggedly. "Where can I fuck you?"

"Balcony," I said.

He shook his head, his hands sliding down my back to cup my behind, pressing me tight against his stiff erection. "You'll scare the birds."

I laughed, and he kissed me hard, dragging me to the couch. This was fine. The desk, the floor. I didn't care. He loved me. We sank onto the small couch, more of a loveseat. He tossed the decorative pillows to make more room. With his hand tangled in my hair, he pulled my head back, licked my throat, and then untied the string that held up my halter top.

Tugging the silky fabric down with his teeth, he nipped at my nipples, making me squeal while my back arched for more. Suddenly, he stopped, looking at me intently, brushing the hair off my face as he searched my eyes.

"I'm sorry I walked away earlier."

I shook my head. "It's not important."

"Yes, it is. I won't do it again. I swear it."

I slid my hands through his tousled, dark hair, tracing my fingers down the bruises on his cheeks and frowning at the memory of watching him take the ruthless beating. He covered my hands with his.

"Don't think about it. It doesn't hurt at all."

With a slow smile, he lowered his head to kiss me. The feel of his body, lips, and hands had always been amazing, but it was different somehow. It felt more comfortable, safer. It was nice being able to take the pleasure he so freely gave and not have to worry about being a sobbing mess the next day.

The short couch wasn't going to be good enough for everything I wanted, so I grabbed him around the waist and rolled us off onto the floor.

He laughed, then groaned when my chin hit his bruised face. "Doesn't hurt?" I asked.

"Shh," he whispered, kissing down my throat. "How many kisses will it take until I'm between your thighs?"

"Make it a lot," I said, closing my eyes, all my nerve endings alive and buzzing for more. How did he bring me to such heights so quickly? "No, better yet, get down there faster."

He chuckled and slid downward, pulling my shorts down as he went, the panties getting dragged along with them. "When I say you have the most beautiful body I've ever seen, you need to believe it," he told me.

I nodded, then gasped when he plunged his face between my legs and instantly found the most sensitive spot. "And the most delicious pussy," he murmured, licking me up and down.

My body trembled in anticipation, the ecstasy building at a fever pitch. As always, I wanted it to last but was greedy for those stellar orgasms he was so good at doling out. Then I realized I didn't need to be so frantic. He loved me. I loved him.

We had all the time in the world to explore each other. What I wanted right now…

"I need a quickie," I said. "Any way you want, but just get that cock inside me."

He looked up from between my legs, seeing my need. As he rose and hurried to straddle me, I told him my revelation, and he beamed down at me. "I like that. Quickie now. Long, slow one bent over your desk in an hour…."

"I suck your—" I gasped when he shoved inside me, deep and hard. "Yes, all of that," I said, unsure if I was agreeing with his plan or urging him on.

"Oh damn," he said as he pumped, his eyes drifting shut as he took his own pleasure from my body.

"What?" I said, panting and digging into his shoulders.

"You can't scream."

It was too late. He rode me to the edge and drove me over, and the sound was already coming out. He smothered it with a kiss, moaning into my mouth as he came inside me.

"Damn it," he said again, his face pressed against my shoulder as his movements slowed. "We forgot a condom again."

"Next time," I told him, trying to catch my breath through the aftershocks. "And the time after that."

We were in love. We had lots and lots of time.

Chapter 28 - Mikhail

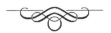

I woke up before the birds and left as silently as a thief from my own house. I had a job to do, and I wouldn't rest until it was done to my satisfaction. Evelina and Leo could crow all they wanted about destroying the Novikoffs in their own way, but I was old school. Digital revenge wasn't enough for me. I needed this finished.

As soon as Evelina was asleep, I searched through her files, finding the name of the elusive Novikoff head, then alerted my driver and bodyguard to be ready. Then I curled up by my love for the hour before I had to leave for New York.

Once there, it was easy to find him. Half his organization was already arrested, the rest scrambling and divided, and my clever girl drained his coffers. All he had left was his luxurious high-rise apartment downtown. He had two guards outside, and I decided to be fair and offer them a choice. Switch allegiances and live or go out defending a dead man.

"Because your boss is going to die today," I told them, training a gun on one while Andre covered the other.

One dropped to his knees and begged for his life. He was currently on probation. Time would tell if he could be trusted to work for Evelina or not. The other one, I had to put a bullet through his heart. His choice, not mine.

Andre kicked down the door and stood back while I dragged the man from his satin sheets and tossed him into the kitchen, where the floor was tiled. No reason to make things difficult for whoever owned this place next.

"You need to apologize," I said.

Despite being in his underwear and on his knees, he looked at me with defiant hatred in his eyes. The feeling was mutual. "For what?" he spat.

I leaned over and grabbed his greasy hair, slamming his head into the granite counter. "You put a hit on someone."

"I put a hit on a lot of people," he said.

I slammed his head again, this time harder. He blinked and looked like he might pass out. No, I couldn't have that. He needed to be aware that he was about to die. "This is the first one on someone I care about."

"Go ahead and shoot me. The crazy bitch already took everything I own."

I slapped him enough to insult him. "Watch your mouth about the woman who brought you to this position right now. On your knees, about to die. Ruined."

I cocked my gun, and for the first time fear entered his eyes. He thought I was bluffing up until now. But I wasn't.

"Look," he said. "Let's make a deal. I still have holdings up in Boston."

I casually checked my phone while still keeping the gun trained on his forehead. "Probably not anymore. Evelina was working on those before she went to sleep last night."

Now that was a bluff, but I had no doubt she would soon have everything under her control, and I wanted him to be good and sorry when he left this earth. If not about what he did, then about what he lost. When he started sniveling, I finished him. I wanted to get back to the woman I loved.

Andre and I wrapped him up in some plastic we found in his own closet and drove him in his own car to one of the bars that Evelina had under surveillance. It was the one that this very man used to hold meetings with his underlings and the one she wanted to use when she took over his operation. There was no doubt in my mind that she could do it, but I hoped to change her mind and choose a different path.

We dumped him on the stoop before it opened. It didn't matter who found him or when. He was gone; that was all that mattered. And Evelina would see it.

"What now, boss?" Andre asked after we left his car in Queensbridge Park.

"Stay and have a little fun if you want," I said. "I'm heading back to Miami as soon as I run a quick errand."

We shook hands and parted like any ordinary businessmen after a breakfast meeting. I caught a cab and instructed the driver where I wanted to go, my mind already on getting back to Evelina.

***

I arrived back at the compound in the wee morning hours, tired from all the travel but quickly rejuvenated when I saw Evelina waiting for me. She sat out on the library balcony in a long, silk robe with a book in her hand, but I didn't think she'd been reading it.

"Miss me?" I asked. "Counting the minutes until I returned?"

She forced a frown and crossed her arms, but a tiny smile broke through her stern expression. "Seeking your own justice?" she asked.

"What?" I asked, all innocence. "Did you see something interesting on your cameras?"

"You know exactly what I saw."

I squeezed onto the big lounge chair beside her, and she scooted over to make room for me. Instead, I pulled her onto my lap. "I couldn't rest easy if I knew he was still alive. Men like that don't give up."

"Unless they're dead," she whispered.

"I would do it a hundred times more," I told her. "That's who I am."

She tucked her head onto my shoulder and snuggled close. "I know that."

"And?" I urged.

She snickered. "And I love you."

"I love you, too, baby. I've been thinking about you all day."

We indulged in a little kissing, making out, and letting our hands roam like teenagers. I wanted to pick her up and take her to bed and waited for her to make the suggestion, but we both pulled away at the same time, both of us seeming to have the same apprehension.

"I don't feel right sleeping in the same bed with you while your father's here," I said.

Her smile was full of relief. "That's exactly what I was thinking. We have our whole lives together. There's no reason to rub it in his face. You know how I—"

"Worry," I finished for her. I had to give up trying to make her see that her father wasn't a fragile old man. He'd beaten the tar out of me after all. My face was still purple and blue to prove it. "Are you going to worry about me like that in ten years?"

She shrugged. "Depends on how much Viagra you need."

I howled with laughter, then squeezed her until she squeaked as punishment. "What kind of joke is that?"

"It's a joke that's meant to tell you I don't care at all about our age difference. Does it bother you that people will think I'm your daughter everywhere you go?"

I was determined to never lie to her. "A little," I said. "Sure. How could it not? Or I'm a dirty old man with a sexy little girl fetish."

She wriggled in my lap. "Maybe this sexy little girl has an old man fetish. Ever think of that?"

"Okay, Evelina. Calm down."

She rubbed her backside over my stiff cock. "Only when you do." She repositioned herself so she wasn't driving me wild anymore. Not as much, anyway. "I hope you can get past it," she said seriously. "The age thing. I hope it doesn't tear us apart."

"I won't let it," I promised. A promise I could keep. "And I'm sure I'll get used to it over time."

"I like this," she said. "Just talking. About real things and the future."

"Speaking of the future," I said, then trailed off.

I couldn't ask her to give up her dreams. I went back and forth between Miami and Moscow for over two years. There was no reason not to rotate them with New York as my main hub if that was where she wanted to be. I'd been living life as a mafia kingpin for more than half my life. It was her turn now.

I pointed to the sun beginning to rise above the treetops in the distance, turning the inky dark sky a vibrant orange and red. "Want to walk in the garden before we go to bed? Separate beds," I added with a sigh.

She got off my lap, and the loss of her warmth nearly took my breath away, but we did have the rest of her lives. I could be patient. We linked hands and tiptoed downstairs, not wanting to wake her father or brother. In the garden, we strolled past the pool, and she stopped, staring at the clear, blue water with an inscrutable look on her pretty face. We'd had a lot of fun the last time we'd been in it together, but then I pulled away.

I had only been thinking about myself then and what a hard time I was having trying to resist her. She had repeatedly offered herself to me, and I had pulled away. Or worse, accepted and then pulled away out of fear. It was time to make her see I was done doing that.

No more waiting. Right now.

Next to a big potted palm, I dropped to one knee.

"Mikhail," she said urgently, dropping down beside me and taking me by the arm. "Are you okay? Did you get hurt in New York and not tell me?"

I started to laugh and kept going until my eyes watered. I loved her so damn much. "Are you already treating me like an old man?"

She stuck out her lip, making me want to kiss her senseless. "I'm treating you like the man I love. Get used to it."

"I plan to," I told her. "Now stand up; I'm trying to do something here."

Her bright green eyes rivaled the trees all around us and widened as she sucked in a breath. Standing, she clasped her hands in front of herself, almost like she wanted me to stop what I was about to do.

"I can wait and do something more elaborate if you want," I offered.

Still rendered speechless, she only shook her head. I reached into my pocket, pulled out the velvet jewelry box, and snapped it open to reveal the four-carat round solitaire. "It's only moderately sized," I said. "But I know you're not showy."

Her mouth dropped open. "It's as big as a Glock bullet," she said.

I laughed again. "That's my girl. Evelina, I love you so much. It's not because you're beautiful, brave, intelligent, or all the other things I admire about you. It's because you make me feel alive. You make me feel like I'm getting a second chance—no, a first chance at love since my first marriage was a bust. Oh, forget I said that. Jesus, Evelina, will you marry me and make my life complete?"

Feeling like I had fudged my speech beyond repair, I half expected her to turn and walk away without a word, but when our eyes met, her face broke into a big, sunny smile. She dropped back down with me and threw her arms around my neck, raining kisses on my cheeks. I held on and picked her up, turning my face until our mouths connected.

"Is that a yes?" I asked.

"Yes, yes, yes," she said, standing back and holding out her hand. "Put it on, please."

I slid it on her finger and leaned down to kiss her again. Footsteps heading down the path made her jump away, and I swore under my breath. I hated that things weren't absolutely perfect.

Oleg burst through the palm fronds hanging low over the path, heavy from morning dew. He wore running shorts and sneakers, a red sweatband around his nearly bald head.

"Morning, Papa," Evelina said with forced cheer.

He gave me a dirty look before turning his gaze to his daughter. She tried to hide her hand behind her back but wasn't quick enough.

"I saw it," he said, his voice devoid of emotion. I never would, but how I want to hit him for erasing the smile from her face.

"Papa, let's talk about this," she said.

"Not right now, Evelina." He continued past us along the path.

She jumped to stand in front of him, holding out her arms, the desperation in her eyes breaking my heart. We'd been so happy ten seconds ago.

"Don't run off," she begged.

"I take a jog every morning," he said, being purposely obtuse.

She straightened her spine and kept blocking the path. "When will you want to talk about it, then?"

His shoulders slumped at her beseeching tone, but he shook his head. "I don't know. I'll be leaving for Moscow tonight. I hope you'll come with me."

"You know I won't," she said, tears welling in her eyes. "But you don't have to go yet, either. You can stay with Ivan or Yuri. Papa, please don't make me choose."

With a sigh, he put his hand on her shoulder and gently moved her off the path. "I will never make you choose, Evelina. I will always be your father, and you will always be my child. But I can't accept this. Not yet. Maybe not ever. But I won't tell you not to choose your own way. I'd rather die than see you unhappy."

With that, he jogged off down the trail, never looking back. Evelina stared after him, then turned to me, her cheeks streaked with tears still leaking from her eyes. My heart ached for her pain, but I feared she'd call things off between us.

"Evelina," I said in a hoarse whisper. "I'm so sorry."

She pressed the heels of her hands into her eyes and then wiped away the tears. "This hurts," she said, holding out her hand to keep me from gathering her up and consoling her. "But I have faith he'll come around. He loves me."

"Of course, he does."

She sniffled a bit more, and her voice broke when she spoke again, but no more tears fell. "I'm going to live the life I want with the man I love. It's the right decision, and everything will work out in the end."

She walked into my open arms, and I held her close. "We have obstacles," I said.

For some reason, that made her laugh, and she looked up at me with so much love in her eyes it took my breath away. "That's an understatement. But I've always liked a challenge."

"I'm right there with you, baby," I said. "Bring on the challenges."

She laughed again and stood on her toes for a kiss. "Together," she said. "For every single one."

Epilogue - Evelina

Three months later

I ignored Leo's call, just like I'd ignored the last one. He knew he was supposed to send me his questions by text because most of the time, I was meeting with florists or trying on dresses and didn't have time for them. I'd be up in New York again in a week, and if there was a real emergency, I would have already known about it. My brother was the figurehead, but it was my operation, and I kept cameras on everything.

It was the perfect compromise. Leo had to expand his horizons and deal with people and not just computer code, and I got what I really wanted most of all in life.

It turned out it wasn't leading my own faction in our family business but being with the man I loved. Mikhail was so supportive; he even offered to move back to Moscow full-time, so I didn't have to give up my detective business.

Once he understood I could do almost everything online, from anywhere, he stopped acting like I was making a big sacrifice for him by staying in Miami. Well, I let him think that sometimes because I loved how sweet he was about it.

As much as I loved the Everglades compound and how romantic and secluded it was, once I started planning the wedding in earnest, no one wanted to drive all the way out there to meet me. It was a huge pain in the ass when I wanted a simple bag of chips late at night. After a few glorious weeks there, like a pre-wedding honeymoon, we had to throw in the towel.

Good thing Mikhail had a beautiful, airy mansion on the waterway, not too far from my cousin Ivan. The views weren't as wild, but they were still stunning, and plenty of wildlife visited the pretty fishing pond on the property. Just not usually the dangerous kind, which was fine with me. The cook who worked for him in the Everglades turned out to be his full-time cook, and she'd grown so adept at traditional Russian dishes that all my cousins and their wives were splitting Sunday dinners between our house and Ivan's.

And it made it much easier for the wedding planner to come and help me understand the seemingly important differences between salmon pink and coral. My maid of honor, Kristina, wanted coral, but my other best friend and cousin-in-law, Kira, thought salmon was more subtle.

My phone rang again. "Damn it, Leo, I'm in the middle of something," I shouted, reaching for my phone. I clamped my lips together when I saw it was my father instead.

"Yes, Papa?" I asked.

Things had been strained between us since he left Miami. I had last seen him when he flew into New York to help celebrate Leo taking over the new territory. He'd almost choked on his champagne, but he'd acknowledged that none of it would have been possible without my hard work. He still refused to speak to Mikhail, but I hoped and prayed he'd come to our wedding. There was so much planning to do it might not be another year which would give him plenty of time to learn to accept us being together.

"I was just looking through an old photo album," he said. "There are some cute pictures of you and Kristina if you want them."

"Sure," I said. "Thanks."

"Do you remember Mrs. Obolensky? Has a daughter your age?"

Ugh, that was Natalia, the girl Leo sexted with. "Yes, I remember her."

"Okay, well, she said that sometimes people put up photos of themselves as kids at weddings. Maybe you'd want to do that."

I was stunned into silence. He'd never brought up the wedding before. I swallowed the lump in my throat to answer. "That sounds like a great idea. Thanks, Papa."

He grumbled. "There's some of you as a little kid with Mikhail, too." My lips pursed. Was he trying to make a point? "Evelina, don't get all pouty," he said, and I loosened my lips. "I'm sincerely trying, okay?"

"That means a lot to me," I told him.

"You mean a lot to me," he said, promptly ending the call.

I swiped the tears out of my eyes, finally brave enough to do the thing I'd come into the bathroom to do.

A few minutes later, I stared down at the double lines on the test. So, this was why I burst into tears at the drop of a hat and had been puking almost twenty-four-seven. I didn't know what to think. Absurdly, my first thought was of Kristina and Kira and all the work they'd been doing to help me plan the wedding. They'd be disappointed to have to cut corners. Then I thought of Papa, who had just shown the first inkling of acceptance. How would he feel about his first grandchild being born "early?"

The door cracked open, and Mikhail poked his head in. "Sorry, are you going to spend all day—" His eyes fell on the test, and he went still. "What does it say?"

"What do you want it to say?" I asked, a new worry added to the list. This wasn't planned. He already had a grown daughter.

He shook his head. "I'll be thrilled if it's yes, and if it's no, we'll just keep doing what we're doing."

"So, you'd be fine with more kids?"

"Kids, plural?" he asked, his eyes widening.

"Well, I'm a twin. Twins run in my family. It's possible."

"So that's a yes?"

I looked at him to see he wasn't scared at all. He looked excited. "It's a yes."

He whooped and picked me up around the waist, then gently set me back on the tiled floor. "I can't wait," he said. "You're happy, right?"

"I really am," I said, realizing it was true. "But, what about the wedding? We can't rush it; everyone will be so disappointed. And I really wanted a ten-foot train. But we can't wait either. My dad would have a heart attack."

He rolled his eyes at my never-ending worry about my father, then snapped his fingers. "Two weddings. A quickie at the courthouse now and a big, lavish affair after the baby's born."

I pushed him out of the bathroom and onto the bed, climbing on top of him. "How are you so smart? And perfect and sexy?"

"I'm only those things because you believe them," he said, wrapping his arms around me and kissing me sweetly. "So, now that we're going to have a baby, do you think I'll be the world's sexiest dad?"

I burst out laughing, loving everything about him and every minute we were together. "Oh, Mikhail, you've always been the world's sexiest dad to me."

His face turned red, but I barely noticed as he pulled me in for another kiss.

THE END

ABOUT LEXI ASHER

Lexi Asher gave up a promising career in the medical field to focus entirely on her family—and her writing. She lives in the beautiful, luscious Virginia countryside with her husband, 3 young children and 4 pets.

The Ashers' rustic cottage is bustling with activity all day long, so when Lexi wants to get her head down and let her creative juices flow, she will often take refuge in their beautifully ornate conservatory where Lexi does most of her writing.

When it comes to love, Lexi is a big believer in second chances—sometimes you just meet the right person at the wrong time. So, her stories often feature old flames that are reignited and broken hearts that are mended. But is love really better the second time around? Well, read and find out!

Books by Lexi Asher

"Morozov Bratva" Series

The Russian Bratva of Miami has three rules: solve problems with violence, paint the streets with blood, and break hearts at will. They're not nice, they're not gentle, and they don't compromise. But behind closed doors, they'll show you what ruthless love really means.

Kidnapped by the Bratva

A Secret Baby by the Bratva

Pregnant by the Bratva

Sold to the Bratva

Forbidden by the Bratva

"Small Town Billionaires" Series
Pretend for the Billionaire

The Billionaire's Baby

The Billionaire's Next Door Neighbor

"The Crenshaw Billionaire Brothers" Series

Billionaire Brothers is where grumpiness and pain give way to romance and love. These loaded heirs may seem to have it all: money to burn, looks to die for, women to spoil. But it takes a special someone, a magical spark to reveal the real man behind the facade.

Grumpy Billionaire

Bossy Billionaire

Daddy Billionaire

"Lakeside Love" Series

Riverroad is a small town where everyone knows everyone, where the guy you've known since childhood turns into the hottest hunk around, where friends become lovers, and where everyday interactions between neighbors might just turn into steamy encounters when you least expect it...

Chasing A Second Chance

Chasing The Doctor Next Door

Chasing A Fake Wedding

Chasing The Cowboy

Printed in Great Britain
by Amazon

39961960R10098